A GIFT FOR ABIGAIL ROSE

Alice Addy

Copyright © 2014 Alice Addy

All rights reserved

2021 Edition

The characters and events portrayed in this book are fictitious. Any similarity to real persons, living or dead, is coincidental and not intended by the author.

No part of this book may be reproduced, or stored in a retrieval system, or transmitted in any form or by any means, electronic, mechanical, photocopying, recording, or otherwise, without express written permission of the publisher.

ISBN-13: 978-1503148888
ISBN-10: 1503148882

Cover design by: Kathryn Klein

Printed in the United States of America

DEDICATION

As I frantically rush about, trying to find that one special gift for the person who has everything, fighting with the ever-knotted tinsel, and failing to locate my Christmas card list from the year before, I pause to catch a breath, and take time to think about the ones for whom I am doing it all for—my family and friends. I am truly blessed to have such wonderful children and grandchildren, not to mention a brilliant husband who loves me, unconditionally. Especially at this time of year, it is important to be surrounded by our family and friends.

Therefore, I would like to dedicate this book to you, my loyal readers, and offer you my sincerest wish for a Merry Christmas and a most joyous New Year.

Alice Addy

CONTENTS

Title Page	
Copyright	
Dedication	
Prologue	
Chapter One	1
Chapter Two	14
Chapter Three	29
Chapter Four	36
Chapter Five	51
Chapter Six	69
Chapter Seven	81
Chapter Eight	90
Chapter Nine	108
A Note From the Author	113
About The Author	115
Books by Alice Addy	117

PROLOGUE

Abigail Rose clutched the small of her back, as she straightened up from making the bed. The colorful wedding ring quilt was showing almost as much age as she; it colors faded and the corners a bit frayed. It had been a valued gift on the day she married the kindest man she had ever known, more than thirty years ago. She carelessly tossed the embroidered pillows across the top of the bed and left the room. There was nothing more to do there. In fact, there was nothing more to do anywhere, but to rest her weary bones and ponder the events of her life.

Recently it seemed there was never a moment when she didn't feel the aches and pains confirming the passage of time. It was funny how feeble she now felt, as it hadn't always been so. Her entire life had been spent working alongside her husband, and keeping up with her active daughter, Patricia Rose. Even though they experienced hard times, those were the happy years. They struggled to get by, suffered with illness and misfortune, but they always managed to make it through to the other side, and always together. They were a close and loving family, and their future looked bright.

Abigail let out a long sigh—a sigh no one heard but the angels in heaven. She was alone now. A single tear ran unfettered down her cheek, as she made her way to the large window facing toward the center of town. It had always been her favorite place, in the entire house, to come and relax; a snug and cozy refuge to rest her body and gather her thoughts, a quiet haven in which to make plans for the following day, and a perfect place to keep an eye on the rest of the world. From her comfortable perch on the window seat, Abigail could observe the goings on of nearly everyone in town, right down the entire length of Main Street, to the bustling town square. Her many friends would smile and wave up at her, as they strolled by, knowing she'd be looking on. Sometimes, they would stop by for a cup of tea and a good long chat. Her very best friend, Libby Long, would rush up the sidewalk, always in a flurry, and while still quite breathless, she would attempt to catch Abigail up on the recent and most scandalous gossip. It was all in good fun, however, and no one was ever seriously maligned. Nevada, Missouri was a nice, quiet place to live.

As in the past, Abigail lifted her long skirt and climbed up onto the window seat; but it no longer felt the same. The joy of happy anticipation was absent. Libby would not be rushing by today. Neither would she see her husband, Patrick, his long legs striding up the front walk, transporting their giggling daughter high upon his strong shoulders. Those were cherished memories from the past and were no longer possible. Today it was mostly strangers that hurried past her window, never giving the old woman a single glance. They were much too busy with families of their own to be concerned with her.

The snow was beginning to fall harder now. The sky had turned a dark, slate gray, and every so often, the wind would whip the new fallen snow into fluffy drifts, blowing into the eyes of the townsfolk as they struggled to finish their Christmas shopping. They had only a few days to fulfill their lists.

Abigail rested her head back against the casement and closed her eyes, listening to the sound of familiar carols echoing from down the street. Happy children shrieked as they frolicked in the snow, throwing snowballs in front of the Mercantile Exchange. It should have been a cheery scene, outside her window, but Abigail only saw those who were missing—the people she loved—friends and family who would be forever absent.

There would be no tree this year, standing in the corner of her parlor. Nor would there be any presents beneath it, as there was no one to open the gifts. She felt the crumpled letter still held tightly in her fist, recalling her daughter's recent words.

"Merry Christmas, Mama. I hope this letter finds you well and in good spirits. Regretfully, I must inform you of a change in our holiday plans. Murphy is changing jobs and being transferred to a new office. He will be getting paid much more, and I am well pleased. While we do not know all the details, it has been confirmed we must move over Christmas week. I know this is disappointing, but perhaps we can all be together at another time soon. Have a wonderful Christmas. Your loving daughter, Patricia."

Each year there had been a plausible excuse for her daughter's unintended absence, but the end result was always the same; simply put, her daughter and little grandson would not be visiting for the holidays—again. Murphy Laughlin, Patricia's husband, was a very successful businessman and could never seem to get the necessary time off from his job, to travel all the way to Nevada. Living so far away, Abigail had not yet laid eyes on her new granddaughter, now six months old.

Unfortunately, Abigail had allowed herself to hope for a different outcome, this year. Now, with the arrival of today's post, she had learned it was not to be. Once again, her dreams had been dashed, and the overwhelming sense of loneliness which permeated to her very bones, had become unbearable.

Having lost so many of her loved ones, Abigail felt she was no longer of any real importance to anyone, and life held little interest for her. There was no one with whom to share her thoughts and desires. Patricia had her own life now, and that's the way it should be, she reasoned. But the constant loneliness that settled over her like a heavy mantle of suffocating misery, was something she could no longer suffer. There were times, in the early hours of morning, Abigail Rose would awaken and not be able to catch her breath—but no one knew—for there was no one to hear her cry out in the dark.

CHAPTER ONE

Nevada, Missouri
December 22, 1897

The silence was oddly comforting. Only the tick-tick-tock of the old mantle clock dared to disturb the absolute stillness in the house. Even the happy sound of holiday revelers had finally abated. Abigail Rose sat on the window seat, staring out through the frosted panes, watching as her neighbors rushed home with packages carefully chosen, tucked safely beneath their arms. Festooned horses pulled sleighs across the hard packed snow, their bells jingling merrily, keeping with the spirit of the season, while Abigail's heart remained as cold and icy as the ground upon which they trod.

Spirit of the season...it was called, but now it was her least favorite time of year. Peering out her window, through the falling snow, she stared at the happy faces of people rushing by with their purchases, laughing and enjoying the company of others. Their bright, shining faces, filled with such hope and good cheer, only served to remind Abigail of all she had lost. The joyous melodies of holiday carolers, singing slightly of out of tune, echoed from nearby. Turning down the lamp, she would rather sit in the dark and revisit Christmases of long ago.

Curled up, with her arms wrapped around her knees and her head resting comfortably against the lovely floral curtains she had so painstakingly sewn, Abigail Rose closed her weary eyes. She gave in to the sweet, soothing balm of sleep, allowing it to settle over her, numbing her senses, and hopefully replacing the pain of the present, with the joys of the past. Her breathing slowed its pace, as her eyelids fluttered slightly; as she began to dream—a beautiful dream of days long ago.

"Oh, Papa, Papa!" Patricia squealed, as she stood up in the wagon, clapping her small hands together, excitedly. "Are we gonna live here, in this beautiful house?"

"We certainly are, Pattycakes," Patrick Donovan replied. It did his heart good to see his precious daughter so happy. In recent years, they had suffered too much, but it now seemed their luck was finally turning around, and he would, once again, be able to provide for his family in a suitable manner. He always believed there was nothing too good for his dear wife, Abigail Rose, and their child. He simply had not figured, on a nation ripped apart by war and all the misery that came along with it.

Surviving the deadly skirmishes was only the first in a very long line of hardships, which they had to endure and overcome. The months of separation were most difficult for his wife, while the years immediately following the civil conflict had been difficult for most Southerners. At war's end, there were too many people left with nothing but the clothes on their backs; hungry and destitute. Farms had been burned and looted, the stock stolen, and jobs were scarce, especially if you were suspected to have been a supporter of the Confederacy. Most everyone just barely got by.

"Will we live here forever and ever? It's the most beautifulest house I've ever seen. Tell me won't never leave, Mama," Patricia pleaded.

Abigail Rose saw the sparkle of hope, in her young daughter's bright eyes, and drew her into her arms, giving her a firm hug. "We're not moving again, darling...I promise. Papa has a good job with the railroad, now. This is truly our home, Patricia...now and forever more...for as long as I draw breath."

"That's all I wanted to know!" the little girl shouted, as she bounded from her seat, practically falling out of the wagon in her zeal to scamper up the walk and onto the wide front porch. "Can I get a dog?" she hollered, as she cupped her eyes and peered through the streaked glass window. "And maybe a kitten, too? And a bird…I've always wanted a bird," she declared, not bothering to turn around to address her parents.

"Slow down, Pattycakes," her father laughed. "Maybe we should get our things settled in before we start acquiring a house full of critters. I'm certain your ma is gonna have a long list of things she thinks she needs as well."

Abigail Rose playfully poked her husband in the ribs. "I have no need of anything, Mr. Donovan. I can make do with what I already have, thank you very much," she smirked.

"Yes, darlin', I'm certain you do, but what about a new hat to wear to church on Sunday mornin'? I wouldn't want the good people of Nevada thinking Mr. Patrick Donovan's wife is too poor to afford a fancy new bonnet, especially on her return to her hometown."

"Well," she grinned prettily, "I suppose a new hat would be nice… but only if you insist,"

"Oh, I do, my love." Parick leaned over and placed a tender kiss upon her lips. "From here on out, I'm gonna pamper both my girls."

"Is there room in the back yard for a pony?" Patricia called out, as she disappeared around the corner of the house.

"Oh, dear," Abigail Rose muttered. "You may have to get two positions at the railroad, darling. It would seem our daughter is expecting quite a lot."

Patrick stepped down from the wagon and reached up to take his wife's small but capable hand. "She's simply excited, sweetheart. Let her dream, if for just a little while, of all the possibilities this move has brought. She'll eventually settle in and rethink her choices. Our girl ain't been raised to be foolish and spoiled. It wasn't easy to bring up a youngin by yourself. This, I know. With me away, fightin', everything was left up to you. And despite it all, you did a good job with her. We will ask her to make a choice between a kitten and a dog. The bird…I'll leave entirely up to you." He grinned, knowing how difficult it was for Abigail to say no to their little girl.

Abigail stepped down and rearranged her skirts. Standing back, *gazing up at the small house with the enormous bay window in front, she could hardly speak. Here, standing before her, was her answer to prayer; and every inch of it was perfect—from the cheery yellow painted siding, to the bright blue door waiting to welcome them home. She wouldn't have changed a thing.*

"Come here, Mrs. Donovan," her husband ordered. "I'm gonna carry you over the threshold, as a proper husband should ought to do."

Abigail laughed, as she struggled to keep away from his long reach. "Don't be silly, Patrick," she shrieked. "People are looking. Whatever will they think of us? Besides, we've been married for years and you carried me over the threshold the night we were wed."

"But that didn't count," he argued. "It was my pa's house...not our'n. Since then, we never owned the place where we lived; we just made do. Some were nothin' more than downright shacks. This is the first real home I've been able to give to you, Abby." He held out his arms. "Let me do this one thing. It would make me mighty happy and I'd be much beholdin' to ya."

Abigail Rose's cheeks turned several shades of pink, hearing her husband's sincere words. She loved it when he called her Abby. It never failed to make her feel like a girl again, filling her heart with innocent joy and total happiness.

Patrick Donovan had always been a good man, and he had tried his hardest to be successful, though luck had never been with him—not until now. How could she refuse his simple request? The neighbors could just go hang, if they were shocked by her husband's actions. "I would be honored to have you carry me into our beautiful new house, Patrick. I only wish there was something I could do for you."

He grinned, causing the pair of dimples in his cheeks to deepen. "Oh, there is, honey. There is definitely something you can do for me... but only after our rambunctious daughter is fast asleep."

"Well, Mr. Donovan," she giggled. "You certainly can turn a girl's head with pretty talk like that."

"I mean to, Mrs. Donovan."

What was that? Was it a noise she heard?

Abigail's heart skipped a beat, as she was startled out from her pleasant dream. Confused, and longing to still be standing in front of her new yellow house, with her handsome husband holding her in his arms, it took several moments for her to realize where she was.

"Oh, it was just a dream," she finally lamented. It was always just a dream, nowadays. Patrick, her dear devoted husband, was gone. He had left her alone, a widow at nearly forty-eight years of age and much too old to make changes or adapt to a new, solitary life. They had been pleasantly married for most of her adult life, and now Abigail was expected to carry on alone—but how? No one could tell her how it was to be done. Her heart felt as empty as a bird's nest in December.

There was the sound again. It was sleigh bells, and footsteps at her back door. Mustering all her strength, she got to her feet and went to investigate. She opened the door just a crack.

"Howdy, Mrs. Donovan," the young man said, as he busily stacked the cut wood.

"Shane Lindell. What are you doin' on my porch? I didn't order any wood from your father."

The boy kept stacking. "No, ma'am, you didn't. It's his way of thanking you for taking such good care of him when he was laid up this past summer. He said the old doc would have removed his leg for sure, if'n it hadn't been for your nursin'. A woodcutter ain't worth much with only one leg. He told me to tell you, you ain't never gonna be outta wood again. He's gonna see you get all you need, winter and summer. This here wood is the best he's got. I'll be bringin' more in February. He sure is grateful to you, ma'am. And so's my ma. She pieced together a cloth for your kitchen table…real fancy, it is. It's in the sleigh. You'd better go inside now, ma'am. You might catch your death. I'll finish up here and put Ma's cloth on your door. Merry Christmas, Mrs. Donovan."

Abigail had forgotten about Mr. Lindell. He had been grievously injured, while sawing wood. It was a miracle she was there and able to stop the bleeding, or he would have lost use of the leg, for certain. She was glad to have helped in some small way. He was a good family man, with eight children, all dependent on him.

Too bad the wood was never going to be used.

"Tell your father I was glad to help. Thank him for the wood." She stepped in and quietly closed the door. She had many good neighbors, but it wasn't enough. She calmly went back to her window seat to dream some more.

As the clock chimed eight times, Abigail stood up on unsteady legs and waited for the room to cease its spinning. *When was the last time she had fixed herself something eat?* Surely, she had eaten a bite at breakfast…had she not? Shrugging away any concern she might have about food, Abigail turned toward the bedroom. It made no difference whether she had eaten or not, she figured; she wasn't hungry now. She would go off to bed without anything more nourishing than a glass of water and be the better for it. She promised to fix herself a bite of toast, first thing in the morning. If she felt like celebrating, she'd butter it and add some jam.

While donning her nightdress, Abigail paused to pick up an old familiar photo of her dear Patrick and sweet Patricia Rose. Smiling, she let her fingers trail over the precious faces of her loved ones. "You did spoil her, you know," she muttered softly, to her husband, as if he could hear her words. There, in the picture, stood her husband grinning proudly, while keeping a firm hand on his little daughter as she happily sat on the pony's new saddle. "You couldn't wait to buy her that pony. Never mind that our land was too small and we had to pay a boarding fee. 'Only the best for our girl,' you always said. But looking back…I suppose it was worth every penny. I wouldn't have changed a thing."

As was her nightly routine, she pressed his image to her lips. "Good night, my dear. I'll be with you soon," she vowed, just before turning down the lamp and crawling into her cold, lonely bed.

Instead of being blanketed in darkness, the room was awash in bright moonlight, reflected off the new fallen snow. Finding it nearly as bright as early dawn, Abigail pulled the quilts up over her head. She wanted to sleep…not lie awake and remember. She had lived a long life, and at times it had been splendid. However, she had been ill prepared for the days of solitude she now faced on a daily basis. Lately, her life had been filled with too much heartache and soul-crushing loneliness. So much so, in fact, she was no longer willing to endure the constant pain. Within the next few days, a week perhaps, definitely before Christmas, she was going to put an end to her worldly existence. All of her affairs were in order. She had seen to that. Patricia would be left everything. She could sell the house for a nice tidy sum, and there was her small savings to be considered. It would all belong to her daughter. Money, photos…yes, and also things, many things…

Finally, at long last, the blessed relief that slumber often brings with it, crept into the room as quietly as fog settles over a valley, and it spread its blanket of warmth over the body of Abigail Rose, soothing her fretful brow and easing her sorrows; welcoming her to take refuge in the more pleasant memories of the past. With one deep exhale of breath, she gave into the invitation and allowed her mind free rein, to wander wherever it desired.

The heavenly sweet scent of spring flowers filled her head, as a warm breeze fluttered her mother's yellow curtains. Outside, Abigail Rose could hear the finches chirping noisily, while two feisty gray squirrels fussed over a scant trail of chicken feed. The month of May had always been her favorite time of year, as the weather was generally perfect; but more importantly, her birthday arrived on the thirtieth. There was always cake and outdoor games to be enjoyed with her brother, Jeb. Barely one year older than she, they had always been inseparable playmates.

Unfortunately, this year would be far different from those enjoyed in previous times, when she was but a child. There had been no war back then, and Jeb had not been away, fighting the killer Yankees. There had been no battle of Stones River, back then.

For more than a year now, the country had been at war, pitting the North against the South, causing each and every person in Nevada, Missouri to suffer the consequences. How many times had she heard her own pa curse the damn Kansas Jayhawkers for attacking another homestead; or saw him get spitting mad at the Cedar County Militia for pushing good folks around, just out of pure cussedness?

Perhaps it was in retaliation for their southern sympathies, or for the part they had played at Wilson Creek; but time and time again, the enemy set upon the good folks of Nevada. Murders, robberies, and acts of arson had become all too commonplace. It was a well-known fact that not a single Vernon County resident had voted for old Abe Lincoln in the last election; nor was it a secret they had organized and fought bravely against the Federal troops at the Battle of Wilson Creek. But that had been at the beginning of the conflict; a conflict that now seemed less likely to result in a Confederate victory. At this point, everyone lived his life one day at a time, waiting and praying for the war to finally come to an end.

"Only five more days, Ma," Abigail Rose announced cheerfully, as she counted off the days on her fingers. "Can you believe I'll be seventeen years old? That's nearly ancient," she lamented, "and I'm still not spoken for."

Since she was a girl of fourteen, Abigail Rose had her heart set on solely one boy, Joshua Benson, son of a nearby farmer. At six foot, two inches tall, the handsome redhead towered over all the other boys in the county, making them appear childish by comparison. He also had the nicest dimple in his chin, which was not lost on Abigail. From their very first meeting, he had succeeded in capturing her heart.

Her mother laughed. It was good to hear the sound of Millie O'Connor's laughter. There wasn't much to be happy about, these days. "Be patient, girl. After this fool war is over, I reckon Joshua will come a callin' fer ya. He's mighty taken with ya. I figure he'll be a talkin' to yer pa the day he comes home."

Abigail frowned. "This stupid old war!" she spit. "I hate it. It spoils all our fun." Suddenly, the insensitivity of her remark resounded in her ears as loudly as a brass gong being forcefully struck. How dare she complain about not having any fun, when her own brother...when her dear Jeb was lying in his grave? She ran to her mother and threw her arms around her thin waist. "Forgive me, Ma," she cried. "I'm awful to speak that'a way. I miss him so much."

Tears rolled down her mother's kind and compassionate face. She was about all cried out now, after hearing the tragic news of her son falling at the Battle of Stones River, and figured it was of no use to cause her daughter to suffer any more than necessary. "That's all right, girl. I know yer a hurtin', too. I only wish we could bury your brother, proper like. I don't even know where Murfreesboro, Tennessee is. I s'pect we'll never know. We can only hope and pray some good Christian woman found his body and buried him, decent."

"Pa told me he was gonna go after Jeb, right after the war is over. He'll bring him home, Ma."

"I pray so, girl." But Millie was nobody's fool. She knew the odds of finding her son's body were slim to none. Most of the Confederate fallen were dumped in mass graves and given no markers of any kind.

Suddenly, the sound of horses being ridden hard, was heard out in the street. Men were shouting orders. Abigail's mother rushed to the window and threw back the curtain. All color drained from her tear-stained face.

"Quick, girl," she shouted, as she ran to bar the front door. "Run out the back and fetch yer pa. Soldiers are a comin'!"

Abigail wasted no time in obeying her mother. Running out the back door and across the yard, she headed for the stable, where her father was busy tending to a lame horse. "Pa! Pa!" she screamed breathlessly. "Soldiers are coming!"

Samuel O'Connor spun around, looking over his daughter's curly head and out past their house, on toward the center of town. Soldiers indeed. Men in militia uniforms were breaking down doors and dragging people out into the street.

"You stay in here, girl," he ordered, and without another word, Abigail's father grabbed his shotgun and made his way back to the house, as she continued to watch in horror.

It wasn't long before the acrid smell of smoke began to fill the air. Abigail could hear the wailing of women and the screaming of their terrified children as they were pulled from loving arms. Frantically, looking around for a place to hide, she rushed to the corner of the barn and knelt behind the feed sacks, curling her trembling body into the tightest ball possible. Covering her ears with her palms, she tightly squeezed her eyes shut, and prayed for a miracle.

That miracle came in the form of two powerful hands, reaching down and yanking her to her feet. "Get the hell outta here, gal," the man yelled, as he shoved her toward the door. "The whole damn town's on fire and yore gonna burn right along with it, if'n you don't get outta here." He gave a quick glance at the beautiful, fragile creature standing before him. With tears glistening in her enormous blue eyes, she reminded him of an angel. It would be a crime if she perished this day. "Git!" he snarled, "or I'll throw you over my shoulder and carry you out like a sack o' feed."

The man was tall and dirty, and appeared not to have shaved in many days. He was a stranger in a scruffy uniform, but as Abigail looked into his face, she saw his eyes were kindhearted and non-threatening. Without hesitation, she nodded once and ran for the door.

Totally unprepared for what she would see, Abigail stopped short, nearly stumbling over her own two feet, as she reached the smoky threshold. It was as if she had suddenly stepped into the fiery depths of Hades. "Everything?" she muttered aloud.

The stranger placed a calloused hand on her shoulder and spoke softly. "It was orders, ma'am. That's all…pure and simple. We have to drive the bushwhackers outta town."

Abigail spun around, anger shooting from her wide eyes. "Bushwhackers?" she shrieked. "Here, in Nevada? I don't even know what that is. You've burned the entire town, looking for something I don't believe exists! How many people have you killed?"

"None, I reckon. That weren't our intent. We allowed folks to empty their homes before we set them alight."

"That was very generous of you. I suppose we should be grateful," she snapped.

"Well, just mayhap you should," he growled. "This here war is gettin' bad, little gal, and I s'pect it's gonna get a whole lot worse for it's over. This ain't gonna be the last time you see soldiers marchin' through yer town.

Abigail knew he spoke the truth. "What town?" she asked incredulously, as she watched men move from one structure to another, setting fire to the roofs and porches. The soldiers were only a few yards away from her own loving home. Helpless to stop the senseless and heartbreaking destruction, her father stood silently in the street, his *arms wrapped around his inconsolable wife. A small pile of belongings was piled next to them, on the ground.*

"If'n I was you, I'd start puttin' some things aside. Hide 'em good, where only you know their whereabouts. Also, some men ain't as polite as me," he warned. "Yer a ripe peach...if'n you get my meanin'. Yer pa needs to take pains to hide you away fer a spell."

Abigail gritted her teeth and straightened her spine. Holding her head high, she turned on the stranger. "I'm not afraid of you or any other stinkin' yankee."

He snorted, not expecting her to be so brave in the face of real danger. "I never said you was, but don't go and be foolish, neither. Heed my warnin', little gal. Take care o' yerself. Go join yer folks now," *the soldier prompted.* "I gotta do this. Ain't got no choice."

"What do you have to do?"

He picked up an unlit torch and struck a lucifer.

"Oh...I see," *she said despairingly. There was no sense in protesting.* "What about Juniper Berry?" *The pony was too old and too fat to be of any use to the U.S. Army, but he meant everything to her.*

"He's tied up out in back. I ain't no horse killer."

"I suppose that's some consolation," *she grumbled.*

The soldier couldn't disagree with the pretty little thing. She had good reason to despise him. Had things been different, had they not been at war, he would have liked to come calling on her. It wouldn't have been so shocking, as he was quite young under all his whiskers —young in years, but terribly old in spirit. Things had changed him. Nevada had been a nice little town, by the looks of it—even if it was filled with rebel traitors and bushwhacking desperados. He hated this war, and he hated his part in it, but that's the way things were; and there weren't no gettin' around it.

"Go on now, gal...git!" *He gave Abigail Rose a gentle nudge toward her parents. They'd be able to comfort her better than he ever could. But maybe, in a few years, he might amble on by this way, and see whatever became of this town and this beautiful girl that lived in it. If'n he could locate her, he might just be able to convince her into steppin' out with him. Maybe she would be able to forgive him for his part in all of this ruin and madness.*

"Oh, Pa," Abigail cried, as she ran into his arms. "I'm so sorry," she blurted.

"Now, now, child," he said, trying to ease her fears. "You got nothin' to be sorry fer. We live in a time of war. There ain't nothin' you, nor I can do to stop this."

"But our house," she exclaimed.

"Them militiamen gave us ten minutes to get everthin' out, we wanted. I reckon we got most of it," he said, as his eyes settled on the pitiful pile of belongings at his side.

The three O'Connors watched as two men, one on horseback, tossed lighted torches onto their house. Within seconds, the fire caught and their pretty little house was engulfed in hideous, roaring, orange flames, the heat searing the family's faces, singeing their eyebrows and lashes.

"Oh, sweet Jesus," her mother suddenly hollered, as she tried to pull away from her husband's grasp. "My quilt pieces! I forgot 'em!"

"Let 'em be, Millie. It's too late, now."

"Noooo," she screamed. "They're in a basket by the door. I can get 'em. We're gonna need the money, Samuel," she insisted, as she struggled to free her hand.

It sure was a sight to see. Mrs. O'Connor bravely running toward her burning house, eyes wild and hair coming undone. "No!" she shrieked, as the hungry flames shot up through the roof, and broke out the precious window glass. Making her way onto the porch, she never once looked back, but foolishly entered the inferno.

Caught off guard, her husband shouted, "Millie! Stop! Come back!" But he was unable to catch up to his wife. Who knew she had such speed?

"Mama!" Abigail cried, as she fell to her knees. "Mama, don't!" she pleaded.

The soldier watched from the corner of the stable, his torch burning brightly in his hand. He could hear the crackling of the flames as they started up in the rear of the barn, the dry wood catching like seasoned kindling. He could hear the frantic neighing of the horse, even though the pony was securely tied to a tree, a safe distance away. However, watching the young girl crumble into the dusty, dirt of the street; hearing her heart-wrenching cries for her ma; was almost more than he could bear. His stomach recoiled, as tears scalded his eyes. More than anything, he wanted to run and lift her in his arms, and tell her things would be all right again, if only she would trust him—but he knew that was just a pipe dream. The young woman would surely hate him now; and she had every right. She would never forgive him for what happened this day, loathing the memory of him for the rest of her life. His heart hitched painfully, as he reconciled himself with the part he played in creating such misery.

John turned away and rejoined his men. They had followed orders and lit the entire town. But he had paid a terrible price as well. Now, there was only one thing left for him to do. It was time to put Nevada, Missouri out of his mind and ride on to another town, fight another battle, and try to see this accursed war through to the blessed end.

CHAPTER TWO

Abigail Rose sat up and wiped the tears from her face, grimacing at the morning light. The familiar dream always ended in the same way. That awful day had occurred more than thirty-four years in the past, and yet the pain of it lingered just under the surface of every day since, fresh and agonizing. The whiff of wood smoke never ceased to bring a moment of aching recollection.

The sudden and unexpected loss of her mother had colored every decision Abigail had ever made. It had influenced the way she treated her husband and the way in which she had raised her daughter. She kept house in a way that would have pleased her mother, and she went to church every Sunday to pray for forgiveness. For deep in her heart, Abigail resented her mother's foolish decision to run back into a burning house for some stupid quilt pieces. True, her ma had earned extra money with her sewing and her fancy quilts, but none of it was worth losing her life and leaving behind a bereaved husband and an inconsolable daughter. For all these years, Abigail had been angry with her mother, and the senseless death that had altered her life forever.

While sitting, gazing down at her tasteless piece of toast and half full glass of untouched milk, Abigail heard a rap at her door. Odd to think, but just a week ago, she might have gotten up to answer it, but not today. Today was different. There was no one with whom she wanted to speak—not in this town, anyway. Perhaps if she sat there, silent and motionless, pretending they didn't exist, they would give up and go way.

"Yoo-who! Anybody ta' home? Abigail?" the voice rang out loud and clear. "I know you're in there, Abigail Rose. I'm not goin' away," the voice insisted. "Open the door, dear, or I'll just come in anyway."

Drat. Why hadn't she thrown the lock? Some folks didn't know when to stay away, and Hannah was just one of those type of folks. She was married to the town's only tobacconist and lived above the fragrant shop. Sensitive to the tobacco scent that stubbornly lingered on her person, Hannah always bathed herself in the most expensive perfumes and toilet waters, and that was a shame, the way Abigail saw it. She had always rather liked the soothing, sweet smell of the pipe tobacco that clung to her friend. It reminded her of Patrick, and of her pa. It was a comforting, manly scent.

"Oh, there you are, dear. Why didn't you answer your door?" A tall, thin woman rushed into Abigail's spotless kitchen, carrying wet snow and a bit of mud with her, as well as the strong scent of gardenias. In her hands, she carried a fragrant pie, still bubbling in the center. "Let me put this down," she said. "I've been busy fixin' pies for the family, and I know I've baked more than we can eat. So I brought you this here mincemeat pie. I remember you said it was your favorite." She smiled sweetly, at her old friend, concerned with the sad state in which she found her.

Remembering her manners, Abigail returned the smile. "Thank you, Hannah. It was very kind of you to think of me."

"Well, of course I think of you. Heavens to Betsy…it's Christmastime! Though a person would never know it by the looks of things around here." Her sharp eyes surveyed the barren room. "Why you ain't got so much as a sprig of holly. Where's your tree… and where's the ribbons and mistletoe you always tie around the chandelier? Don't you always bake up a big batch of sugar cookies to give to the carolers? I don't smell 'em bakin' in the oven, and them folks will be mighty disappointed if they don't get 'em. Your lemon drop cookies are the talk of the town. What's wrong, Abigail? Won't you tell me? I'm worried about you. Ever'one is sayin' as to how you ain't been yerself, lately."

Abigail took a deep breath. She was too worn out to explain, and no words could adequately describe how she felt. Perhaps she could say she had given up on life, but that was too simple. Maybe her friend would understand better if she explained about the many losses in her life being too much for her to bear. Then there was the deep sense of loneliness she felt, every time the morning sun shone through her bedroom curtains. Everyday was always the same, with her being of no value to anyone, anymore. Living a life with no real purpose was impossible to endure. But this was Hannah…and she had the attention span of a fly.

"I've been feeling a little old, lately. It isn't anything for you to worry yourself about, Hannah." There was, after all, nothing the woman could do to change matters. Life was what it was, and there was no going back.

"Oh, good," Hannah exclaimed, obviously relieved that her friend would not be needing for her assistance. "I'm glad it's nothin' serious. I've got too much to do, as it is. Is Patricia coming home for Christmas?"

"No, she—"

"That's too bad. A daughter owes it to her mother to visit her at Christmas time…at least that's what I think. My Louie is comin' all the way from Topeka. Will you need help with your tree this year?"

"No, I don't expect—"

"Thank goodness. I'd have offered to help you, but I'm just so busy. It's Sol's busy time of year, you know, so that man's absolutely no help at all around the house. I have to do everything, if it's gonna get done."

As quickly as she had blown in, Hannah spun around and headed for the door. "Well, I'm glad to see you're doin' okay, Abigail. You need to get out more. You look kinda' peaked. Cut yourself a big slice of that pie. It'll put roses back in your cheeks. Merry Christmas, Abigail. You can return my pie tin next Sunday, after church."

Abigail sat numbly, listening for her front door to open and close. "Merry Christmas," she mumbled in return, as she continued to stare at the steaming pie sitting in the center of her table. It was true. At one time, a fat slice of mince pie had been her favorite. Now, it held no special meaning for her. It was nice of Hannah to think of her, however. She would have to remember to leave her friend a note, one that would explain everything. She would want to thank her for her kindness.

Abigail stood up and carried her plate to the garbage bucket. The toast slid off the plate and joined the toasted cheese sandwich from the day before. She managed to finish the glass of milk, and set it in the sink. The tasty pie would have to wait for another time.

The rest of the day was simply spent going through the motions—anything to pass the time—all of it routine. Make the bed, sweep the floor and shake out the rugs, before fixing the midday meal. Then do up the dishes, dust the tabletops, and plump the pillows. Once a week, she would also clean the windows and sweep the porch, but not in weather such as this.

All too soon, there was nothing more for Abigail to do but sit in her favorite chair, stare out the window, and be alone with her thoughts. Letting out a long, troubling sigh, she allowed her gaze to drift about the room, taking in one thing after another, ascribing a precious memory to each item. Every piece told a story—the story of a young woman desperate for the security of a home and a family to call her own. Someplace safe.

This cozy old house had always been Abigail's personal sanctuary. Whenever there was trouble, something too difficult for her to face alone, she knew she could find peace within these sturdy walls. Images of another house, long ago set afire, the sound of her mother's screams, and the anguished cries of a man unable to save his wife, were put aside; in this house, she could smile and carry on.

Abigail was well pleased with the beautiful floral paper still covering the parlor walls. The colors had not faded much over time, although it was beginning to curl in one corner. She remembered with fondness, how her husband had fussed about its feminine colors and disturbingly large cabbage roses, peeking through white latticework. He declared it was enough to give a man nightmares, and he threatened to send it back to the warehouse in Chicago, requesting a refund of his money and demanding they not accept any additional catalogue orders from his mentally deranged wife. In reality, as soon as the first garish roll went up on the wall, and he saw the ecstatic joy it brought to Abigail's face, he knew he had no choice but to resign himself to living in a woman's frilly front parlor. At least he didn't have to sleep there, he had grumbled, good-naturedly.

Soon after the wallpaper was hung, Abigail busied herself with the making of ruffled curtains, to be hung inside the large bay window, and the sewing of matching pillows for the settee and padded window seat. Even after years of laundering and ironing, they appeared nearly as good as new. The fabric had not aged and the tiny stitches had held up well.

Tall cut-glass vases, which now stood empty, had once held a variety of colorful and fragrant flowers from her garden, and were perched on every table. Her neighbors and friends had always insisted she had the sweetest smelling parlor, of all of them.

Abigail wiped away an errant tear. Those were golden days. They had many friends then, and were active in the church. Patrick was by her side, and her daughter, Patricia, was young and full of life. They had been truly blessed.

Reaching out to touch a small, brown and white dog figurine, Abigail lovingly stroked it between the ears. She remembered when her husband purchased it for their daughter. Patricia had broken her leg, and was miserable, confined to her bed. With nothing much to occupy her time, he figured she might take pleasure in gazing upon the little spaniel's funny, painted face with its pink tongue hanging to the side. The special gift worked like magic. Patricia was once again happy and glowing with good health. When walking past her open door, they could hear her confiding to her little porcelain friend, giggling and whispering secrets into his long wavy ears. Time passed quickly, and long after she left her sick bed, "Curly" oftentimes accompanied her, hidden safely away in her pocket.

Curly was to be the first of many lovely bone china miniatures, strategically placed here and there, all around the house, each one special and unique. In Abigail's opinion, she had the most beautiful parlor in town, and it made her smile, each and every time she laid eyes on it.

An unexpected knock brought Abigail out from her pleasant reverie. Who would be disturbing her now, she muttered to herself? If only she could ignore it, they might just go away—but it hadn't worked with Hannah. Slowly, she got to her feet and trekked to the front door.

Pulling it open, she came face to face with an exceedingly cheerful woman, bedecked in her splendid holiday finery. Refusing to give into her desire to quickly shut and bolt the door, Abigail remembered her manners. Unable to stifle a small groan, she did her utmost best to sound cordial. "Gladys...what brings you to my door? It's cold enough to freeze a person through and through."

"Uh, y-yes it is, Abigail R-rose. Might I c-come in for a s-spell?" she stammered, wide-eyed, with teeth chattering; hoping for a warm fire and a cup of hot tea.

Abigail stood firm, blocking the door. "I was planning on taking a nap, Gladys. I'm not feeling very well, today."

"Oh, I hope it's n-nothing serious. Should I s-send for Dr. Graham?"

A slight twinge of guilt began to nibble at Abigail's conscience. She wasn't ill—not exactly—and now her good friend, Gladys Archer, would worry. "It'll pass, Gladys. It isn't anything for you to worry about. Now, go on your way," she prompted.

"I could c-come in and fix you s-something hot to drink," she offered hopefully. Maybe she could fix something for herself, as well. Bending down, to pick up a rather large basket hidden behind her skirts, she cheerfully announced, "As luck would have it, I have b-baked you a chicken and made a bowl of delicious dumplins; light as a feather they are, too. It should t-taste mighty good on a r-raw day such as this. Oh, p-please, Abigail Rose," she pleaded, "can't I c-come in for just a few minutes and thaw out?"

The small, annoying twinge was threatening to grow into a rather large, stabbing portion of guilt, for Abigail. Her good friend had brought food, and was simply begging for a little warmth, and she was considering turning her away. *Why was everything so difficult?*

"Now why did you go and do something nice like that?" she grumbled. "I got nothing for you. I haven't been up to seeing folks, lately, and I've been stayin' in. In fact, I'm thinking about not celebratin' Christmas at all, this year. There's no point to it. Now, you take this basket over to Marvin and Calvin's place. Those two old fools don't have any womenfolk to cook them a good meal. They need it a sight more than I do."

Gladys took a step back, her face flushed with more than the frigid temperature. "I swear, Abigail Rose...I don't know what's come over you. Hannah told me you were not yourself, and now I have seen it with my own two eyes. You are most definitely not well. I'm going to f-fetch the pastor and have him come by, presently. He'll get to the bottom of what ails you. F-furthermore, my dear friend, I will n-not take your refusal of this basket to heart. It is quite delicious, if I must say so myself, and I made it especially for you. The S-stark b-brothers will receive one of their own. I'll leave yours here, on the porch, by your door. You can ignore it and let a perfectly good chicken go to waste, or you can take it inside and enjoy it; knowing it was b-baked with a great deal of love. Who knows...you might have an unexpected guest to feed. You never know."

"Now, Gladys Suellen Archer! Don't you speak to me thataway. If I don't want to eat it...then I don't have to. No one's comin' to my house for Christmas, and that's a fact. I have no need for your charity."

"Charity!" her friend screeched. She couldn't believe her friend was even thinking something so outlandish. "You couldn't be further from the truth. This isn't charity. Have you forgotten my first Christmas here, in Nevada? I had n-nothing...absolutely nothing but my pride, mind you. You were the only one to notice my predicament, and you came to my rescue without me asking for it. F-food, medicine, clothing, and a r-roof over my head, you saw to it all. If it hadn't been for your kindness, Abigail Rose, I would surely have perished that first winter. You even introduced me to my beloved husband. The way I see it, I owe everything I have to you. Now take this d-damn basket. I've got more places to go and important things to do than standing around here, spreading Christmas cheer and freezing my butt off."

Abigail didn't know what to say, so she held out her hand and received the heavy basket. "Thank you, Gladys. Merry Christmas," she said in a small voice.

Gladys planted a soft kiss on her friend's cheek. "Don't you know we'd all miss you, if you was g-gone? It just wouldn't be the same. Merry Christmas, my dear friend."

Without another word, the lady in the bright red cape and white fur hat and muff, turned on her heels and was gone, leaving deep tracks in the snow. She wasted no time in making her way toward the little run-down cabin at the edge of town, intent on delivering another basket of Christmas cheer to two old crotchety brothers, Marvin and Calvin Stark. Hopefully, she would be able to warm her feet and hands in front of their fire.

Abigail closed the door quietly, and carried the heavy basket into the kitchen, where she placed it in the center of the table, right next to the untouched mincemeat pie. For several minutes, she just stood there, staring at its gaily-wrapped contents. Not only was there a plump baked chicken and a covered jar of dumplings, but she saw a jar of green beans & ham, as well. Under a clean dishtowel, were a plate of sugar cookies and a loaf of light bread, no doubt as tasty as any cake. It was a complete meal; and a terrible waste, she thought, as no one would be there to eat it.

After having put the carefully prepared dinner away, Abigail made her customary rounds of the silent, empty house. It was getting late, and the snow continued to fall, casting a blue tint to the evening light. By now, the townsfolk had finished their daily toil and labors, and had locked up their shops and businesses along Main Street. Even the carolers had gone home to rest their voices for another day of holiday warbling. It was a time to make peace with the day that had run its course, and prepare for the new day yet to come. Abigail was prepared, and the time had arrived for her to carry out her plan.

She didn't bother to light a fire. It wouldn't warm her anyway. Her insides were frozen, as if already dead and buried beneath the snowy white mantle of winter. She looked around the cold, lifeless bedroom, of which she had once been so proud, but now which only brought her despair, and she was confident she had made the right decision. This would be her last Christmas.

Abigail had prepared everything the best she could. Her jewelry, what little there was of it, was left to her daughter, Patricia, and was carefully tucked inside the wooden box Patrick had so lovingly carved for her, their first Christmas together, as husband and wife. He had worked on it for weeks. Abigail remembered how he had laughed about it then, apologizing for the fact that the jewelry box was empty, but vowing to someday fill it to overflowing. He had done well, by his vow, and there were many precious items safely stored within it's velvet interior. Her granddaughter, Isabella's, new dolly was in her box, wrapped in bright, store bought paper and tied up with string. She had wanted to get a fuzzy bear for her new grandson, but had not been able to get out of the house long enough to purchase it. Sadly, the baby would never know his grandmother. There was also a well-worded letter for her good friend, John Douglas, the only attorney in town, bequeathing everything she owned to her only child. She was satisfied her affairs were in order.

Although she would rather not use her small, pearl handled derringer, a gun was so loud and messy; poison was out of the question. She needed to be quick about it, before she lost her nerve, and ingesting arsenic or drinking lye was too horrible to contemplate. Yes, it must be a bullet.

Raised a Christian, and going to church nearly every Sunday of her life, the act of taking one's own life was against everything she had been taught, and that bothered her a great deal. She had prayed long and hard about it, agonized over her choice. Would God forgive her? Would He have mercy on her soul? She did not know, but held onto the fact that He was a merciful Lord and knew how badly she was hurting. Surely, He would want her misery to end.

If she were intent on doing this, she was determined to make as little work for those she left behind, as possible. Walking over to her wardrobe, she pulled out her best dress. It was a deep shade of purple, with delicate lace stitched around the neck and cuffs. The petite ceramic buttons, running down the front, were decorated with tiny flower blossoms, painted by an artist, and imported from Paris, France. She fingered the smooth, glassy surface. They had been a terrible extravagance, but Patrick had insisted nothing was too good for his wife. Abigail wiped a single tear, as it made its way down her face.

"I guess this'll do for my buryin'," she murmured softly, laying it out on the bed, smoothing away any wrinkles.

She gently placed the precious jewelry box alongside the dress, with a note attached for Patricia. The doll's box was placed next to it. She had written letters to her loved ones, explaining to the best of her ability why she did what she did, and wishing them the very best. It would be her Christmas sentiment to them—her last. Hopefully, it would soothe old wounds.

Yes, everything was almost ready.

Her hand shook, as she picked up the cold, steel derringer. It felt strangely heavy and foreign in her palm. Looking at it, she realized once the trigger was pulled, there would be no turning back; she would be ending this life—forever. How had she gotten to this point? When had God abandoned her? When had everything gone so terribly wrong?

In years past, she would have started preparing for Christmas in August, secretly sewing and creating presents for each of her loved ones, and for the underprivileged as well. There was never a needy child, nor an elderly person in all of Nevada, forgotten at this time of year. By December first, all her plans would be ready to go.

Now, however, it was all just a hurtful memory. No longer was there anyone to sew for, or to cook for, or even to share the beauty of a tree. Her brother, Jeb, loved Christmas, as no other, always singing and whistling, whilst preparing to eat himself nigh onto bursting with holiday vittles. For many years now, his cold body had rested between limestone outcroppings, in amongst the cedar trees, in a place called Murfreesboro; Tennessee, she had learned. Having taken a musket ball to the chest during the second battle of Stones River, he had died Jan. 2, 1863; just a few days after Christmas, and only a few months before their mother was struck down defending her own home from pro-union militia, as they torched the entire town of Nevada.

At the sudden and grievous loss of his wife, her father, Samuel O'Connor enlisted in the Confederate army, leaving his daughter to care for herself. Several months had passed since Lee surrendered to Grant, and Abigail clearly remembered the day she learned of her father's fate. It was a dark morning; the clouds seemed to weep over what was left of her house and town. A man with a knapsack entered on horseback. He had been a good friend of her father's, and had promised to return his private journal to his daughter. According to him, her father had been taken prisoner during the siege of Vicksburg and had been transported north by train to a Federal prison. It was there he contracted pneumonia and died. Although feverish and struggling for each breath, he continued to smile. His last thoughts were of his wife and child, and his home in Nevada.

Abigail was left desolate and alone, but nothing quite broke her heart as much as hearing of Joshua Benson's fate. He had been a prisoner of war for more than a year, kept in one of the country's most despicable and dreaded prisons...Andersonville. Having fought for the North, he was eventually released, only to perish on the steamboat, Sultana, while making his way toward home at war's end. It was a needless tragedy for thousands of families, one that probably could have been prevented.

Unlike everyone else around Nevada, Missouri, Joshua had

chosen to wear a blue uniform and fight for the Union. More importantly, he had promised to marry Abigail as soon as the war was over. Getting down on one knee, he had lifted her hand to his lips and asked her to wait for him.

Naturally, she did as he asked, even though some townspeople cautioned her, saying he was a traitor and no good. But their words held no meaning for her. She didn't give a fig what color he wore, she just wanted to see him again, and have him kiss her face and stroke her hair, and tell her he was home to stay. The war had ended. He should have been safe.

However, the country was tired of fighting a most gruesome war, and President Lincoln had just been assassinated. The horrible tragedy that occurred in the early morning hours of April 27th, 1865, in the murky waters of the Mississippi River, just above Memphis, barely caused a ripple in the newspapers.

Abigail sighed, remembering his sweet smile and the deep, comforting timbre of his voice. Always an easy one to laugh and forever willing to listen to the ramblings of a young girl, Joshua's demise left her heart tattered and torn. After losing him, she could not imagine ever falling in love again, but she was wrong

Who would have thought the tall, lumbering man from the next county over, would come in and manage to steal her heart? It wasn't the exciting, passionate love, she had experienced with Joshua, but it was solid and comfortable, nevertheless. When she gave herself to Patrick Donovan, it was forever—until death parted them. And it had been an excellent match. He had been an exceptional husband, loving and supportive. Looking back, there was no doubt they had had a good life. Years later, when Patrick, the man she vowed to love through good times and through bad, passed away in his sleep, she thought she could not endure the pain and loneliness that surrounded her. His death had been totally unexpected, as he was never sick, and she had been unprepared. One evening, he was there enjoying his supper, and then he was simply gone before breakfast. His last words to her were complimentary. He had run his fingers through her hair, now streaked with silver, and declared he was a lucky man. "I married the prettiest gal in the entire county," he boasted. "And she just gets prettier with time."

She swatted his hand away, and called him a silly old man, but her eyes sparkled with the love she had for him. As always, they kissed before getting into bed and turning down the lamp.

"Good night, dear," she had whispered.

"Mmmm," he had sighed, wearily. "Sleep tight, my love. Wake me in the mornin'. Got lots to do." Within seconds, his breathing had turned soft and regular. It always amazed Abigail how quickly her husband could fall asleep, as it sometimes took her hours to find peace. Oh, how she wished she had stayed awake that last night. Perhaps she could have prevented his slipping away.

Soon after Patrick's death, their only child, Patricia, had married a stranger from Richmond, Virginia, and had decided to live there. Abigail soon discovered her daughter was not one for writing letters, and she seldom heard from her. Over the first year, she had received only three letters, in fact, and was feeling cut off from the only family she had left. Her son-in-law had invited her to come for a visit, but that was out of the question. While not really poor, circumstances had dictated she be thrifty, and the cost of a railway ticket had prevented her from making the trip. To this day, she had not seen her newest grandchild, Isabella Rose, named in part for her. And she doubted her little grandson, Connor, would remember his grandmama. He had just cut his first tooth, when they decided to move away. Abigail sighed. The boy had resembled his grandfather in so many ways. It always warmed her heart to see his sweet smile.

Looking back over the years, Abigail realized she had had more than her share of misfortune, but she had also experienced great joy, as well. A wonderful marriage, a beautiful daughter, and many good friends had filled her days. Her health was decent and the roof over her head didn't leak. All in all, she should not be contemplating ending it all. So why was she turning the small gun over in her hand?

It was the pain of recently losing her best childhood friend,

Libby Long, which had brought her to this fateful decision. She couldn't remember a time when Libby wasn't in her life. In fact, it had started when they were just babes. After Libby's ma came down with the fever, she was no longer able to nurse her tiny infant. Her husband feared the child would die; she was so small and frail. As the little girl child grew weaker, he frantically went from house to house, farm to farm, in search of a woman capable of nursing his baby. Abigail was only four days old when Mr. Long came knocking at their door. Her ma said it took only one glance at his sad and fearful face, to know she had no choice in the matter, and he could not be turned away. From that day forward, little Baby Long, lived in the Donovan household, sharing a fine wooden cradle alongside a bawling Abigail Rose.

So it was with the little girls. Their lives continued to be inexplicably entwined. Sadly, the very day Abigail lost her mother, Libby lost her father. When Patricia Rose Donovan entered this world, Libby was by her best friend's side. She fussed over the child so, one would think she had given birth to her. Then Abigail was there to hold Libby's hand and wipe her cheeks as they entered her little twin boys into the tiny grave. They had gone through everything together. Good times and sad times, too. They always had each other to lean on...but no longer was that true. One day, Libby was full of energy and good health—the very next... she was lying lifeless, at the foot of the stairs. She had tripped over her new slippers; bright yellow slippers she had crocheted for herself, and of which she was so very proud.

The moment Abigail laid eyes on her dear friend, lying stiff and unnatural, on a bed of satin, Abigail realized she was now truly alone, perhaps for the first time in her life, and try as she might, she would not be able to separate herself from the feeling of total despair. Her sense of bereavement was so complete it controlled her thoughts, night and day. Lost and confused, she turned to her faith for extra strength, only to discover her prayers had fallen on deaf ears and gave her little comfort, leaving her with an agonizing choice. Everything in life had led her to this moment.

Turning down the lamp, in an attempt to shroud the distasteful deed from any well-intentioned neighbor's watchful eye, and keeping it confined to the shadows where it belonged, Abigail walked slowly toward the table. Her hand shook as she lifted it to the lamp. Just as her fingers grasped the key, a slight movement from outside her window, captured her eye, causing her to pause for a moment and peer out onto the lawn. Something definitely stirred in the darkness.

"This will never do," she grumbled to herself, frustrated by the unexpected delay. How could she fire the derringer, knowing full well someone was standing in her yard, only a few feet away from her window? Hearing the gunshot, they would no doubt be alarmed and run for help. She had no choice but to send this meddlesome person on his way, before carrying out her final decision.

CHAPTER THREE

Usually, at this hour, the entire house was enveloped in a peaceful blanket of darkness, providing Abigail with some security from prying eyes. She was used to the inky shadows that jutted out from the walls, and in fact, much preferred the blackness to the harsh light of day. Not bothering with a lamp, she felt her way through the familiar parlor, crossed the dining area, and entered into the kitchen. The floor was surprisingly cold beneath her bare feet. Only an hour before, she had been standing there, broom in hand, and a small fire still glowing in the cook stove. For some irrational reason, she had refused to leave her house in anything other than pristine condition. It would not be said Abigail Rose Donovan left dirty dishes in the pan. She had swept the floor until it shone as bright as a new pin. It had felt considerably warmer then. The outside temperature was obviously falling, and therefore could be blamed for the sudden frostiness, causing a chill to run up her spine. It was going to be a frigid night, and the sooner she shooed this person away, the sooner she could get on with her task.

Abigail had no idea who would be standing in her yard at this time of night, but whomever she expected, she was totally unprepared for what she discovered. To her utter amazement, huddled up against the porch railing, she found a small, trembling child—a boy, to be exact—only he was unlike any child she had ever seen. His flaxen hair was dirty and matted, his feet were bare, and his enormous eyes drooped down at the corners in a perpetual look of sorrow. Unusually captivating, his sad, mournful eyes seemed to grab at her heart. She found it hard to breath, in his presence. Lashes, so long they seemed to flutter in the wind, as they caught the heavy flakes of falling snow, framed blue eyes so pale they appeared almost silver. Such unusual eyes. They seemed to captivate.

There was something even stranger about him, however… something quite astonishing. As she stood observing the poor child, unable to move her feet or even speak, Abigail's eyes began to burn with an overwhelming sense of awe; as if she was secretly gazing upon something no mere mortal should see…a celestial being…or a wee angel, perhaps? Was he sent from heaven? It was Christmastime, after all.

A boy of such unusual beauty certainly did not belong to this cruel world, but here he was, nonetheless, and Abigail felt she had no choice but to come to his aid. No matter his origin, boy or angel, he was in desperate need of her help. Suddenly, and unexplainably, a surge of golden warmth rushed in to the very depths of Abigail's body, forcing out the glacial emptiness that had taken up permanent residence deep inside her heart. Abigail could feel the icicles break away, making room for something else.

The thought then occurred to her that perhaps this child's sudden appearance was not accidental; it could be he was sent to save her. But it also might be a total coincidence the child sought out her porch in an effort to find refuge from the snow. Surely, she was reading too much into all of this. Everything was suddenly turned topsy-turvy. This poor child had no idea what his unexpected arrival had done to her well-laid plans.

"My stars!" she gasped, after finally finding her tongue. "You're just a boy. What on earth are you doing out here on my porch…and on such a terrible night as this?"

The boy said nothing but continued to focus his enormous gaze upon Abigail.

He was small and fragile in appearance, poorly dressed and underfed. No older than six or seven years of age, he was dressed in nothing better than rags, and was nearly frozen stiff. No shoes were on his scruffy little feet; no soft woolen scarf was wrapped around his neck to protect him from the wintery winds that stirred the snow in ever swirling patterns over the hard, frozen ground. His delicate flesh had taken on a pale blue hue and was so papery thin his tiny veins were visible just under the surface. He said not a word, but with a single look from his enormous eyes, he conveyed his extreme need, and captured Abigail's very soul.

Unable to avoid looking into those fathomless eyes, Abigail was shocked by what she thought she saw. It must have been a hallucination, the beginning of a fever, perhaps, for she thought she saw the joy and the pain of the entire world through his eyes; all the love and goodness that resided on earth, as well as the lost hopes and unfulfilled dreams of its people, rested there. Happiness and despair were present in those innocent eyes. As a shiver ran up her spine, Abigail realized it was as if she was staring into the eyes of God.

She gasped, fell down on her knees, and began to weep.

Without a sound, the child came to her and took her hand, leading her back toward the comfort of her home.

It was very much like a dream. Nothing seemed quite as it should. Shaking her head in disbelief, not certain as to how she got back inside her house, Abigail lowered her eyes and took a good long look at the little ragamuffin standing with his hand pressed in hers. One minute they had been outside, the cold air chilling them to the bone...and the next she discovered herself standing here, in the relative warmth of her kitchen. It didn't make much sense, but then very little had made sense, this night.

"What am I doing standin' here, askin' you a bunch of fool questions?" Abigail blurted out, her voice weak and unsteady. "I'm wastin' valuable time. You're froze half to death." Removing her heavy woolen shawl, she threw it around the boy's thin shoulders, engulfing him well within its luxurious folds. It was soft and warm, and smelled as clean as mountain air.

Placing his face in the shawl's softness, appreciating the comfort of the garment, the boy found joy as the curly yarn tickled his nose, bringing a small smile to his face.

"You go on in and sit down, little fella. We'll get you warmed up right quick. First, you'll eat something...and by the looks of you, it's not a minute too soon. It's been a long while since you've had a decent meal, I imagine. I'll fetch you some clean clothes, and you can spend the night in Patricia's bed. She's my daughter, but she don't live here anymore. You don't got nary a thing to worry about, little fella. Abigail Rose will take good care of you...just wait and see if I don't."

Remaining silent, the child decided to put his trust in the pretty lady with the sad eyes, and allowed her to hustle him over to the kitchen table, all the while making a big fuss over him. She sat him down and quickly poured a tall glass of milk, then rushed off to find him something warm for his feet, still shockingly blue from the frigid temperatures outside.

After only a few minutes, Abigail rushed back into the kitchen, her blue eyes sparkling, as they hadn't in a very long time. In her arms were various items of clothing. "I got some nice wool socks that should be perfect for your feet, and I grabbed a flannel gown from my daughter's closet. It's a mite girlish, but I didn't figure you'd mind, bein' frozen and all. I found you a clean hairbrush and another pair of socks. Tomorrow, I'll see that you get some proper clothes...more fittin' for a boy. I'm gonna see that you get everything you need." Abigail paused, glancing from the boy to the now empty glass of milk. That's when she noticed he hadn't uttered a sound.

"You don't talk much, do you?"

He shrugged his shoulders and gave a slight smile, revealing a wide gap in his front teeth. All the while, his luminous eyes continued to communicate something to Abigail, arousing something inside her she thought was lost or destroyed over time. What was it about the child that made her want to rejoice? He was definitely poor—probably an orphan—and she very much doubted she would be allowed to keep him. And what had happened in his life to cause him to choose not to speak? Had his pa beat him? Had he at one time fallen ill with a fever? The entire situation was profoundly too sad to contemplate, but oddly, she didn't feel sad at all. In fact, it was quite the opposite. This felt like a heaven-sent opportunity. Finally, there was a purpose to live—at least temporarily—and for as long as this precious child needed her, she vowed to do her very best by him.

"Whilst you climb into these clothes, I'll heat up some chicken and dumplin's. My good friend, Gladys, made them, and she's the best cook in town. If you're still hungry, I'll slice up a delicious piece of mince pie. Does that sound good?"

The child's forehead wrinkled, while the corners of his mouth turned down in distaste.

"What? Don't tell me you don't like chicken and dumplin's or mincemeat pie? I've never heard of such a thing."

The boy slowly shook his head.

Abigail thought for a minute. Perhaps he was one of those religious folks who didn't eat meat. "Eggs?" she tested.

Again, he shook his head.

"Oh, dear. I suppose bread and jam wouldn't tempt you either."

Suddenly, the little boy's entire face lit up, smiling from ear to ear. Nodding enthusiastically, he sat up straight and licked his lips in anticipation.

Abigail clapped her hands together. "That's it, then. I'll fix you some of the best light bread you ever tasted and slather it with my blue-ribbon blackberry preserves. Now, you go on and get dressed, while I slice up the bread."

After six generous slices of bread were devoured, and four tall glasses of milk had been consumed, Abigail suggested it was time for him to go to bed. He was just a child, and he had had a tough day. Together, hand in hand, they shuffled off toward the bedrooms, his pink ribboned gown trailing behind him and his socks working their way down his skinny little shins. His face had been scrubbed, leaving his cheeks pink and shiny, and his hands had been washed clean of the dirt and debris carried in from the outside world. For the first time, in a long time, his tummy was full, and a contented smile was plastered across his angelic face. All was finally right with the world, this night. Or at least, that is what Abigail thought.

As they passed her room, the child suddenly snatched his hand back and pulled away. Without looking back, he stepped through the doorway and approached the bed.

"No, little fella!" Abigail exclaimed. "That's my room. You'll be sleepin' in the next room...my daughter's room. Come away from there." A feeling of dread slowly crept over her. "No! Don't go in there!" she shouted abruptly. She was afraid for him to see —but it was too late. The child stood transfixed at the foot of the bed, staring down at the hideous object lying on the quilt. Turning his head, he appeared to stare straight through Abigail's skull, wordlessly accusing her of something horrendous. Slowly, he raised his arm and pointed directly at the small derringer. He required an explanation.

Embarrassed beyond measure, Abigail reached for the corner of the quilt and hastily tossed it back over the offensive object, hiding it from view. Mortified that he should see and suspect its real purpose, Abigail reached out for him, and felt his frail body shaking violently, as a river of tears pooled in his enormous eyes and spilled down his cheeks. "Please, child. Don't be afraid. It's only a wee pistol I keep in my drawer. I'll put it away. It won't harm you."

A deep sense of sorrow and condemnation emanated out from him, charging the air with a bitter energy, which could only be described as divine judgment. Although the child remained speechless, it seemed to Abigail he was shouting his disapproval loud and clear, denouncing her plan to exit this world voluntarily. Never in Abigail's life had silence been so deafening.

With her knees threatening to give way, Abigail knelt beside the small boy and coaxed him down onto her lap. She felt him relax, bit by bit, as he rested his head against her breast, quietly sniffling. Running her fingers through his platinum curls, she began to slowly rock back and forth, the way she had when Patricia could not sleep, and found herself humming one of her favorite lullabies. His breathing slowed, becoming regular, as his innocent eyes grew heavy, finding it impossible to stay open. It wasn't long before the young boy was fast asleep, snoring in the way that baby's do. Abigail let out a long sigh. For the first time, in a very long time, she felt the true weight of what she had planned to do. Through the eyes of this child, she could now see the pain her suicide would have inflicted upon others—those whom she claimed to love more than life itself, and those she wanted so desperately to protect. It was a cowardly and selfish thing for her to do. Guilt overwhelmed her, but relief was there, too, for she had a second chance; a chance to make things right. Suddenly, she saw things for what they truly were. Life was a blessing and a gift; and if she was to spend her remaining years alone, she would live it to the fullest; to the benefit of others…and she would start tomorrow.

CHAPTER FOUR

It was a glorious morning. The sun shown almost blindingly bright, upon the snow that had fallen overnight. The glistening icicles, hanging from the roof overhang, were beginning to melt, lengthening to enormous proportions, and folks, clearing the sidewalks, were waving and calling out to friends and neighbors. Something special was in the air, and Abigail Rose knew what it was.

She stood in the doorway of the boy's bedroom, watching him sleep. A sweet smile was on his lips and his eyes darted back and forth behind closed lids and long lashes. He looked like a cherub, lying there so peacefully. Although his flesh was still startlingly pale, he appeared to be in good health. Abigail felt her heart swell with love for this foundling. She would offer to help him find his folks, but she silently prayed he would be with her until her dying day. This child had already been a blessing to her, and she wanted this marvelous feeling to continue.

The boy began to move under the quilt, stretching his arms above his head, at which time his eyes popped open wide and he stared directly at Abigail. Then a smile stretched across his face, nearly from ear to ear.

"Well, good mornin'," she exclaimed. "Did you sleep well?"

He nodded and pulled the covers up to his chin.

"It's nippy in here, but I'll have the fires goin' in the blink of an eye. Breakfast is nearly ready. As soon as you're dressed, come into the kitchen. We've got a lot of things to do today. It's a right pretty mornin'…so skedaddle. You'll have to wear this here dress of Patricia's. I hope you don't mind, but I ain't got nothin' else for you to wear, and you can't go shoppin' wrapped in a blanket. After you eat, we'll go to the mercantile and get you some pants and shirts. Does that meet with your approval?"

The boy sat straight up and smiled once more, his blonde hair bouncing with each exuberant nod of his head. He threw back the covers and put his little feet on the cold floor.

"Good," Abigail declared. "Don't forget to put on double socks. Can't have your toes falling off."

She thought it impossible for his eyes to grow any larger, but that's just what they did. He was wondering if it was possible for his toes to actually fall off.

"Don't worry about it, little fella. I'll take good care of you. Now, get dressed and I'll see you out in the kitchen."

◆ ◆ ◆

The soft wool surrounding his skin felt good. He didn't mind that he looked more like a little girl than himself. The pretty woman was kind and doing her best by him. He could see the sadness in her eyes, and hoped that it would lessen in time. Although he was just a child, he knew the significance of finding the small gun lying on her bed. She had tried to keep it from him, but she was too late, and what he had seen filled him with heart wrenching sadness. He had seen this before and the outcome was always tragic. This lady deserved more than that.

Abigail tightened the soft knitted scarf around his neck, and then stood back to admire her efforts. "Well, my stars…you're almost as pretty as my Patricia was when she wore that coat. Of course, she's a full-grown woman now, with children of her own. You know, I've never even seen my little Isabella Rose—that's the baby. She's named for me. I have me a little grandson, too. His name is Connor Murphy Laughlin. He must be about four years, by now." Her eyes grew misty and her voice softened. "I miss my babies. It's been such a long time…"

The little boy grabbed her hand and pulled her toward the door. His brows rose expectantly, making Abigail laugh. ""You've got it right, little fella. There's no time for reminiscing or feeling sorry for myself, we've got much to do." Abigail reached for the door and swung it open, instantly feeling the bite of the clean, frigid air against her face. "After we buy you some clothes that fit, how about us making a stop at the sweet shop? I can guarantee they have something that will cause you to roll your eyes with pleasure. You'll think you're in heaven."

He nodded, ready to start their day.

"Another thing," she said, as they stepped off the porch, their breathing creating frozen puffs in the air. "I can't go on callin' you 'little fella', or 'boy'. No indeed. We need to pick you out a real fine name. "I've always been partial to Michael. How's that?"

They hurried along, passing the Tobacconist, the Leather and Harness shop, and Ruth's Millinery, before the child halted in front of the Nevada Emporium. He was gazing most earnestly up at Abigail.

"What is it, Michael?" she asked.

He frowned and shook his head.

"You don't like the name Michael? Is that it?"

He nodded, solemnly.

Thinking it important that he should approve of his own name, Abigail proceeded to find a more suitable name. "John? Patrick? That was my husband's name, you know." The boy slowly shook his head from side to side. "Well, then...how about David or Ezra? Elias? William?"

Several minutes later, Abigail was still reciting familiar names. "I'm afraid I've plum run out of names, child. I don't see nothin' wrong with any of them, but I suppose a man is entitled to his given name. Can you write it down?"

The boy shook his head, as his bottom lip began to quiver.

"Now don't get upset. We've got lots of time to find your chosen name. Right now, it's more important that we get you some decent clothes. I'm about to freeze to death, standin' out here on the sidewalk. Let's get you inside and warm you up by the stove."

The little boy nodded eagerly, leading the way through the door, causing the over-the-door bells to chime loudly. He stopped abruptly, and looked up at the shiny brass object above his head. It was obvious he took great pleasure in the sound of it, as he opened and closed the door behind them, repeating the process several more times.

Abigail quickly scooped him up and plopped him down again, directly on top of the enormous polished counter.

"Miss Abigail Rose!" the man exclaimed. "Come in. Come in. It's mighty good to see you again. Sure is. I heard you was feeling poorly, but you look a beautiful sight this morning...fine as a new fiddle, in fact. What can I do for you, madam? Need to finish up on some Christmas shopping?"

Abigail's cheeks turned deep pink, remembering her original plan for the holidays. Hopefully, the kind man would think her blushing was a result of the wintry air, and nothing more, for she did feel a great sense of guilt for worrying her friends. She had willfully, and with no explanation, stayed away from them, causing them a great deal of concern. But far worse than that, she had contemplated...No! She would not allow herself to go there in her head—not today. It would ruin everything. She would not recall the dreadful, dark days just prior to discovering the little boy, half frozen on her porch.

"It was kind of you to be concerned, Mr. Cheney, but as you can see for yourself, I am much improved. In fact, I have a little visitor for the holidays, and he is in serious need of a new wardrobe."

For the first time, the man took notice of the thin, frail child sitting on his counter. He could only stare, as the child's silvery blue eyes took measure of him. The boy was entirely too young to have eyes so wise; they were slightly unsettling. The clerk moistened his lips and tried to gather his wits. The lad was dressed most pitifully, more like a girl than a boy. Wearing a girl's coat over lacy drawers and old boots, several sizes too large, he resembled a poor blonde waif, left alone to freeze in the snow. The jolly old man chuckled good-naturedly and held his hand out to the child. "Hello, son. I'm Mr. Cheney, and I own this store. What do they call you?"

The boy looked at Abigail.

"Luke," she said emphatically and without hesitation. "His name is Luke."

The child smiled broadly, and bobbed his head in agreement.

"It's surely good to meet ya, Luke," the cheerful man said, sincerely. "I'm glad you've come to spend some time with this nice lady. She's had a run of bad luck lately, and we've all been a mite worried about her. But I guess she's in good hands now...am I right?"

Luke nodded.

This wasn't the introduction Abigail had anticipated. Something extraordinary had just occurred, but she wasn't certain what it was. Glancing from one to the other, it seemed as if Mr. Cheney recognized this boy. What did he understand that she did not?

Alton Cheney did not know why he felt so reassured in the presence of this child, but there was something about him that put his fears at ease. Such a small child, but one filled with a strong spirit capable of caring for a lost soul. It was Christmas... perhaps this child was an angel, come to save Abigail Rose. He had heard of such things.

Abigail squared her shoulders and pulled her shawl tightly around her shoulders, feeling a sudden chill in the room. "Luke needs everything, Mr. Cheney. I would appreciate it if you would take him under your wing. I know very little about boys. In the meantime, I will do some shopping at the mercantile." Cupping her hand around her mouth, Abigail whispered, "Christmas, you know."

The storeowner winked, conspiratorially. "Ah...yes, I see. Naturally, I'd be happy to fix this fine lad up with all the necessities. He'll be the best dressed lad in town."

"That sounds perfect," she remarked. Giving Luke a chuck under his chin, turning his face up to meet hers, Abigail grinned and said, "I'll only be gone for a little while. After you're finished here, you and I will go to the sweet shop, just as I promised. You'll be all right here, with Mr. Cheney...yes?"

Looking somewhat concerned, Luke barely nodded, but gave her a small, pathetic wave goodbye, doing his best to be brave. Abigail couldn't resist the sudden maternal feelings that sprung up inside her. She spun around and ran back to his side, where she wrapped her arms around him, giving him a strong hug and a kiss on both cheeks. "Look at us," she laughed. "I'm only going to be gone for a few minutes and we act as if we're never gonna see each other again. That's not going to happen, Luke. I promise to come right back. Now, you be good a good boy and let me go."

Luke giggled and happily waved her on, watching as she left the store, the door jingling merrily, as it closed behind her. He finally turned around to Mr. Cheney, cocked his head, and put his hands on his hips.

"So now you're ready, are you?" the proprietor teased.

Luke nodded, and pointed to a red plaid shirt with sparkling metal buttons down the front and fancy stitching across the chest.

"Fine choice, son. Fine choice."

◆ ◆ ◆

Abigail Rose sat in amazement, watching Luke drain his third cup of hot chocolate. She would be surprised if his frothy mustache had not permanently attached itself to his upper lip. But it was a good feeling, seeing the little boy so happy and content. All traces of fear and sadness had left his wondrous eyes, replaced with the excitement and magic of the season that only children could sense. And her own heart was lighter. *When had that happened?* She knew it was only temporary and that her plans had only been delayed for a couple of weeks, but Abigail Rose couldn't help but smile. Luke was special, indeed, and had taken up residence in her heart...even if only for Christmas.

"You look mighty handsome in your new clothes, Luke," she

declared. "Did you pick them out yourself?"

The boy sat up straight, puffing out his small chest. Smiling, he pointed out the fancy buttons and stitched pockets. Grinning, he jumped down and stuck out one skinny leg, showcasing his brand new boots and trousers. Never had he worn anything so grand.

"Like I said," Abigail repeated, "you're looking mighty good in your new duds. And that wool coat is going to keep you warm all winter. Maybe Santa Claus will bring you some gloves and a scarf to go with it." Her eyes twinkled, knowing she had all the makins' of both, in her bag. It was almost like knitting for Patricia again. There was real joy in creating something for someone in need. The yarn was dark blue and it would be edged in brilliant red. Festive, but useful all winter. "If you're ready to go, I think it's time we made our way back home. The sky is growing darker and the wind has picked up. I wouldn't want you to get blown away."

Luke chuckled, and placed his napkin on the table, next to the empty plate of cookies. He reached for Abigail's hand, and once again, she felt her breath hitch and her heart stumble. Luke made her feel grateful to be alive. At least for the time being, she was needed and inconceivably happy.

"Let's go, Luke. We've got a lot to do, if we're going to be ready for Christmas."

Luke nodded, and pulled Abigail toward the door.

Only steps away from Mr. Cheney's store, Abigail heard the voice of a boy, calling out her name.

"Miss Donovan! Miss Donovan! Wait up!" A tall, and much too thin, boy reached her side, by the time she halted. His ribs were heaving up and down, trying to draw breath. He had been running to catch her.

She recognized the voice, immediately. The face was familiar, although a bit more mature and a great deal dirtier than the year before. "Gabe, is that you?"

"Yes, ma'am," he said breathlessly. "It's me, shore 'nuff."

"My stars...I haven't seen you in quite a while. You certainly are shooting up. I believe you'll be fully grown, by this time next year. How are your mother and sisters getting along?" Everyone knew the family was nearly destitute. The boy's father had run off with a no-good redhead from Kansas City, and never once looked back at the sweet family he had abandoned. Although the little family tried their very best to make a living, luck was never with them. Sickness plagued them, regularly. Abigail suspected it was because of their unfortunate circumstances. The lack of good nourishing food and a leaky roof over their heads was a frequently discussed topic amongst her friends, but Gabe's mother was a proud woman and refused any kind of charity, insisting on providing those things, the best she could. It was only through indirect means, that she would accept any gifts from her neighbors.

Gabe was the eldest son and tried so hard to be a man at twelve years old. Industrious, he always had some way of making a little extra money. "I got ya somethin' here," he wheezed, fishing around in his feed sack for something special. "I made it special for you, Miss Donovan…somethin' fer yer Christmas." He pulled out his hand and presented to her a shiny tin star. "You can hang it on yer tree or in yer winder. It'll catch the light, I s'pect."

Abigail took the slightly misshapen ornament and held it up to the sun's bright rays. It was obvious the child had made it with a great deal of difficulty. Its edges were sharp and ragged. "Why, it's beautiful Gabe. How did you make it?"

He shrugged his shoulders, but was clearly pleased with her praise. "Outta some ol' tin cans I found out back of the hotel's kitchen. It ain't stealin'. They don't care if'n I take a few."

"Well, I should hope not. You're doing them a service. These are actually quite lovely, Gabe. How much do you want for it?" She knew his family needed the money. Last year, he sold walnut halves, crudely painted inside and out, ready to adorn a tree. The stars were much superior.

"I was hopin' fer a penny. Is that too much?"

"Well…I don't know. I figure it took a lot of time to snip and shape into a Christmas star. And by the looks of your fingers, you were wounded more than once, in the process." He had more rags wrapped around his bleeding fingers than he had covering his nearly bare feet.

The boy hid his hand behind his back.

"I think maybe it's worth a whole dime, Gabe."

The little boy about fell over. He didn't figure his whole bag was worth a dime. "Thank you, Miss Donovan. I'd like to give you another one," he said, thrusting his hand back into the bag. "Ow!" he yelped, as he quickly withdrew his fingers, blood running down his wrist. A tin can ornament had sliced deeply into his palm.

"Oh, my goodness, Gabe...you're hurt! Come along with me back to Mr. Cheney's. He'll be able to fix you up, right quick. Luke will carry your bag. Won't you, Luke?"

The young boy nodded, as he had already retrieved the sack of tin ornaments from the snow and had thrown it over his thin shoulders. His forehead was creased with concern for the boy called, Gabe. He knew the boy's life was unduly harsh, and it probably wouldn't be much of a Christmas for him, or his sisters.

One glance at Gabe's tearful face, and Alton Cheney called out to his wife. "Florence! Come quick and bring the tincture. We got us a bleedin' boy out here!"

Within seconds, Mrs. Cheney entered the front of the store, carrying a bottle of salve and a clean towel over her arm. A cheerful woman, almost as wide as she was tall, she was known to be sweet and considerate. "Oh, you poor thing," she fussed. "This'll sting a bit, but you're a brave lad. I can see that. We wouldn't want your hand to get the gangrene, now, would we?" She took his hand and held it tightly against her body, as she poured the treatment over the gaping wound. "The doctor would have to cut it off, you know."

"Florence," her husband scolded. "The boy's scare enough as it 'tis."

She blushed a bit, and gave a wink to her patient. "I could sew it up for you," she offered. "The doctor couldn't do no better."

"No!" Gabe shrieked. "I mean...I'm much obliged, ma'am, but I don't mind a scar. It's only a scratch...honest!"

She chuckled, seeing the fear in his big eyes. "Well, maybe it isn't so bad, after all, but you'll have to promise to keep it clean, or the doctor will have to look at it. Let me see under all those dirty bandages, you've got. Are you hiding more cuts that need tending to?"

"Maybe one or two," he mumbled.

Luke plopped the feed sack down on the counter, spilling its contents for all to see. Gently, he picked up a shiny disc and tossed it high into the air, causing it to twirl and shimmer in the light.

"What's that you got there, Luke?" Mr. Cheney asked.

"Gabe has been making these beautiful ornaments to sell. I bought one, myself," Abigail confessed. "I offered him a dime for it." Without saying another word, speaking only with her eyes, she conveyed her concern for the boy's family. Who knew if they were warm enough, or if they had enough funds to afford good food? Surely, Christmas presents were out of the question. Although Gabe's venture was less than totally successful, the effort he put forth in the creation of these tin stars was commendable.

"Ah, yes, I see." Alton scratched his chin, while surveying his big window. "You know…I do believe I could use something to catch the shopper's eye in my front window. Your stars might be just the thing, Gabe." He glanced over at the boy with the smudged cheeks. Having his cuts cleaned and bandaged had been a painful ordeal, and he was having difficulty keeping back the tears. "Would you think of sellin' me your entire sackful of ornaments for…say, three dollars?"

Three dollars? Gabe had never dreamed he'd be offered such an enormous sum. That was more money than he had ever seen. He'd be able to give it to his ma, and watch her smile. She didn't do that much, anymore. His little sisters would have meat and eggs to eat, and maybe something sweet. Suddenly, the tears were impossible to hold back, as they overflowed his eyes, creating muddy tracks down his face. "Th-that's more'n there worth, mister, but you can have 'em fer three dollars…and the sack, too. I never had no idea a man could be so…so…" Gabe wiped his wet nose on his sleeve, purely overcome with gratitude.

Abigail felt her own tears flow warm down her cheeks. It was a wondrous sight, seeing this young man's simple expectations met with such generosity. After a few moments, she felt a soft tug on her sleeve.

"What is it, Luke?" she sniffled. The boy pointed to Gabe's bare feet.

"Mr. Cheney? I would like your opinion. Do you think shoes or boots are the most practical for my Luke?"

"Huh?" What was Mrs. Donovan asking, Cheney wondered? From out of the blue, she was asking about shoes and boots? Then he noticed young Luke staring at Gabe's shoeless feet and understood. "Well, now let me see. Luke is wearing shoes...and they're the best I got, but I'm a mite partial to boots. Longer wearin', I'm a thinkin'. Why do you ask?"

Abigail grinned slyly. "I'm not entirely convinced. But if you could find someone willing to test the boots, I might be persuaded. Do you know anyone who would be willing to wear a pair of the boots? They would have to promise to be hard on them, put them to good use."

Mr. Cheney snapped his fingers and looked directly at Gabe. "What size boot do you wear, Gabe?"

The boy shrugged his shoulders. "Don't know. I ain't never had no new boots, before. I guess my feet are smaller than yours, but bigger than Luke's."

The old man chuckled. "That makes perfect sense. Son, if I allow you to wear these new boots, do you promise to be tough on 'em? Don't save 'em for Sunday go to meetin'. Mrs. Donovan needs to know if they're sturdy. Are you willin'?"

Gabe nodded enthusiastically. What a lucky day he was having. Three dollars and a new pair of boots to keep for his very own? He had to pinch himself to make sure he wasn't dreaming.

"Well, find and dandy. It's all settled. I'll fix you up with a pair of new boots, and you will come by the store next summer and let me know if they need to be stretched or replaced. It's important we test these boots." He figured the boy would need a size larger, come summer.

Abigail threw her arms around Mr. Cheney's neck. "You are a wonderful human being, Alton Cheney. If there's anything I can do to repay your kindness, you just ask. There are some people who keep Christmas, every day…and you're one of them. God bless you," she murmured. "Now, it's time for me to take Luke home. He's exhausted." His eyes were still shining, but they were growing heavy and he needed the counter for support.

"You run along, ma'am. The wife and I will gladly see to Gabe. Merry Christmas, Abigail Rose. Merry Christmas, Luke."

◆ ◆ ◆

After a short nap, followed by a satisfying supper of flapjacks, lighter than air, swimming in rich, creamy butter, with plenty of maple syrup poured over the top, Abigail felt it was the perfect time to show Luke her daughter's secret place under the stairs. Not much more than a cubby, it was nonetheless, Patricia's favorite place in the entire house. In it, she would play house or read a book, teaching school to her imaginary friends. Sometimes, she just chose to nap with her favorite doll. When they played hide and seek, she always ran there, knowing her mama and papa would never find her. Of course, they never did. Abigail smiled.

To this day, it was just as her daughter had left it; filled with games, dolls, and colorful wooden blocks, her papa had made for her. He had sanded them all with care to alleviate any sharp edges that might splinter. Abigail then painted each one in a beautiful color, with a design on every side—snowflakes, flowers, rabbits—everything to make a little girl smile. The colors were now rubbed thin from sticky little fingers, covered in raspberry jam. Patricia built castles, villages, and forts, but her favorite thing to do was stacking them as high as herself, and then watch them begin to teeter. Holding her breath, biting her lower lip, she would add just one more to its towering height, then squeal with delight when it collapsed, scattering blocks all over the rug. Only once, had her papa accidentally found an errant block with his bare feet. After limping to his chair, he gave it a toss and told her he had discovered the one that gotten away. Instead of feeling remorse for being the cause of her papa's pain, Patricia ran to him and threw her chubby arms around his neck, thanking him for finding her most favorite block. She promised to scold the naughty orange block and swore it would never run away again. Her papa was the very best papa in the whole wide world, she had exclaimed. Many years later, they had a good laugh about the incident.

It had been a long time since Patricia visited the magical oasis. When she left home, after marrying, and felt she no longer needed these childish things. She was content to leave them there, gathering dust and cobwebs. The thought of it nearly broke Abigail's heart, and had only added to her sense of loss. Now, because of Luke, all that had changed and she couldn't wait to share this secret playground with him.

The hinges had collected dust, and creaked as she lifted the latch, opening the oddly shaped door, revealing a tiny, but surprisingly well-stocked child's nook. Abigail stood back to give the boy room to survey its contents. In the center of the space, there was a small chair to sit upon, and a colorful rag rug covered the cold floor. A candlestick was attached securely to a shelf. Box after box was filled with the most wonderful items; toys of every description were neatly stored away, waiting for another child to come and discover them.

Abigail heard a soft gasp of surprise and astonishment.

"Well...what do you think, Luke? I know it could stand a good cleanin', but it's filled with many valuable treasures," she said, recalling the numerous hours her little Patricia had spent there, lost in her imaginary world. "I'm sure you can find something to while away the hours. Go in and have a closer look," she urged.

Luke entered the tiny place of astounding wonder, slowly, as if he wasn't quite certain what to expect. In all his days, he had never before seen anything like it—not even back in Norway. Even Mr. Cheney's store paled in comparison. There were painted horses carved from wood, and soft, flannel dolls with smiling faces. A large dollhouse stood against the inner wall and a red barn sat beside it, filled with animals of all kinds. Storybooks were piled in a corner, while chipped cups and dishes rested in another.

A yellow and green spinning top rested on its side—right next to the popgun and slingshot. He looked back to Abigail, silently inquiring.

She laughed. "Patricia could be as rowdy as any passel of boys. Her father taught her how to shoot a tin can from nearly thirty feet away, before she was seven. I think I could recommend a book you might like, or maybe I could get you interested in a good game of checkers. I used to be fairly adept, in my day."

Just as Luke reached for the checkers, his eye fell on something tucked in a tattered basket. With a little effort, he managed to dislodge the item. Holding it up to Abigail, he held his breath in expectation. He just had to have it.

"My stars...you found Clementine," she exclaimed. "I thought she was long gone. Patricia looked everywhere for her, but she never found her. I can't believe she was here, all the time. Would you like to have her, Luke?"

The little boy looked down at the fragile wooden donkey he held tightly in his hand. Its paint was worn thin, one ear looked as if it had been chewed upon, and its entire tail was missing; but yes, he had to have Clementine. He nodded and held the toy close to his heart.

"Clementine was part of a simple crèche," Abigail explained. "Patrick worked on it for months, carving each piece with care... all for his little girl. I never saw a man dote more on his child, than my Patrick. I don't know whatever happened to it all. I suppose it wore out, piece by piece, and was tossed away. Patricia loved it so. For hours, she would lie on her stomach, under the tree, and move the pieces around from Judea to Bethlehem. The three kings would come riding in and have a tea party with Mary and Joseph... but not the baby Jesus. He was too little, she'd say." Giggling at the absurd memory, Abigail was forced to wipe her eyes. "I imagine this little burro is the last surviving piece, so she's very special, indeed. It's really a shame, though."

With one hand clenched firmly around Clementine, Luke reached out with his other hand and gently patted Abigail on her arm, as if to say he realized the importance of this small, wooden figure.

Abigail's heart melted. He was such a sweet and caring child. It might have been selfish and wrong of her, but more than once, she had silently prayed his folks would never come to claim him. What would she do then? The small derringer was now and forever out of the question, which left many years of loneliness ahead of her. "Please, Lord...if it be thy will, let me keep Luke, always," she muttered softly.

She straightened to her full height, and smiled down at the little boy engrossed in another basket. "Well, I'll leave you here to play for a while, but it will soon be time for bed. 'Early to bed... early to rise', smart folks always say. Tomorrow will be another busy day for us. There are only four more days until Christmas, and I must start my baking. I give pies, cakes, cookies, and such to my neighbors, and to those who are in need of sweet treats."

Luke looked up and held up his fingers, pinching each and every one.

"Yes, dear. We won't forget Gabe and his family. Tomorrow, you can help me cut the cookie dough for their special cookies. They'll be a surprise and twice as tasty, knowing they came from friends. It will be a wonderful day, Luke...simply wonderful.

CHAPTER FIVE

Abigail stood back, admiring her little companion in his fancy new duds. It seemed as if Luke had always belonged with her, just as if the child was meant to be standing in her kitchen, doing exactly what he was doing. The little boy made the picture complete for her. His face was all spit and polished, and his beautiful blonde curls were under control, at least for the moment. Fancy new boots kept his feet toasty warm, while Abigail's checkered apron kept his shirt and trousers flour free. He had discovered the joy of baking. But most exciting of all, he had discovered a bag of cookie cutters, low on a shelf in the pantry. A rearing horse was particularly nice.

"That was my daughter's favorite, as well," Abigail remarked. "I was partial to the bell. Patrick always chose the snowman. He'd bite the head off, and then eat the middle section, leaving the bottom for last."

Luke giggled. The morning had been perfect. Sweet, delicious aromas filled the house, mouth-watering cinnamon and nutmeg filled every corner. It was fun to play with the horse and snowman, and it was nice to see the happiness in Mrs. Donovan's face.

"Not too much sugar, Luke," Abigail instructed, knowing how he loved lots of the sweet stuff. "We're going to ice these, and that will make them very sweet. Do you need help rolling out the dough?"

He happily shook his head. This was his third batch of

cookies, and by now, he was feeling quite confident in his efforts. He floured the rolling pin, the table, his hands, his nose, his sleeves…the air he breathed…

"Bless me, child," Abigail exclaimed, as she waved her hands in front of her face. "A little flour goes a long way, Luke. It will take us a month of Sundays to clean this kitchen." Suddenly smelling the heavenly scent of brown sugar, drifting up from the oven, she ignored the current flour storm and quickly removed a tray of hot, golden cookies from the oven.

"Perfect!" she announced. "We'll let them cool, and put the last batch into the oven. You'll have enough cookies to last you through January. Now, I'll show you how to make the icing. It's sweet…you'll like it."

Only after everything was baked and decorated, and the kitchen cleaned with all the dishes put away, did Abigail bring down a very special tray. She removed a soft cloth, covered in dust. It had been years since she had used the lovely old dish. It was so precious to her, the weight of it caused her hands to tremble. After all this time, her heart would surely break if anything were to happen to it. With great ceremony, she gingerly placed it in the center of the kitchen table.

"This was my mother's dish, Luke," she proudly declared, letting her fingers lovingly trace the green holly border painted around the edge. "It is one of the very few things I still have of hers. Our house was burned, you see, and nearly everything in it was lost. It was a time of war, and we could save only what my father was able to carry out on his back. For some unexplained reason, as he was running through the burning house, he stopped long enough to take this beautiful bit of porcelain down from its shelf, on the hutch. It was her mother's, before her…very old and very dear. After my mother's death, and my father had gone off to fight in the war, I cared for the tray the best I could. It never had its own place, but I managed to keep it in one peace," she said tenderly. "There's a number of things I have misplaced over the years…things I would like to see one more time before I die; but it's too late now, I reckon. As the years roll on, things tend to be pushed aside or discarded altogether."

Luke ran to the sideboard, where the cookies were resting, and returned with a bell covered in white icing. He placed it gently in the center of the platter, then stood back smiling.

Abigail wiped an errant tear from her cheek and put her arms around the small boy. "That's right, Luke. This platter is for our Christmas cookies. We'll pile 'em high and watch them dwindle, as we celebrate the holidays. We'll probably get the bellyache, but I s'pose it'll all be worth the misery," she grinned.

Just then, Luke cocked his head and ran to the large bay window in the parlor. Abigail could hear the distant voices of carolers outside her house. They were filing up her walk, singing louder as they advanced. "Oh, no," she muttered.

Luke spun around, his face brightly beaming, as he ran for the door.

"No, Luke!" Abigail Rose shrieked. "Not this year. I'm just not up for it." But the child did not hear, or he chose to ignore her refusal, and threw open the door. He jumped up and down, clapping his hands and motioning for Abigail to join him. She had no choice but to greet her uninvited visitors.

The harsh wind blew past the little group and through the open doorway, blowing Abigail's skirts up around her ankles. The harder it blew, the louder they sang, and before the second verse began, she discovered she was quietly humming along with them. Hearing the well-known hymns, lifted one's spirits and one's voice, it seemed. Happily singing The First Noelle, Abigail failed to notice Luke leave their gathering and disappear from the parlor. At the conclusion of the song, Abigail politely applauded and stepped back, preparing to close the door.

Luke suddenly came bursting around the corner, and caught his toe on the threshold, which caused him to fall face first onto the rough porch floor. He fell hard, and the beautiful porcelain plate, which he held in his hands, skidded across the snow covered boards, coming to rest against the wall.

"Oh, no! My plate!" Abigail instinctively cried in alarm, right before her eyes landed on the poor little fellow lying face down in the snow. "Luke, darling…are you hurt? My poor boy, can you get up?" she pleaded; fearing he may have hit his head or twisted a limb.

Luke was slow to get to his knees, but he appeared uninjured. It was only then, that Abigail Rose looked at her mother's lovely platter. She couldn't believe her eyes. Miraculously, not a single cookie had been disturbed, nor was there so much as a tiny chip on the plate. The heavy snow must have cushioned its path.

"Can we help you, Mrs. Donovan?" a woman asked, as she bent over to retrieve the exquisite platter. Abigail discovered it was Gabe's ma, and she had him and his two sisters in tow. Standing behind her were the two old, crotchety brothers, lending their fine tenor voices to the chorus. With tears in her eyes, Abigail smiled, feeling very foolish to be worrying about a plate. Glancing down at Luke, rubbing both his knees, she nearly cried. "Yes, as a matter of fact, you can do something for me. I reckon you have sung enough for the time being. Now, it's time to come inside and get yourselves warmed up. It's cold enough to freeze your breath."

"And our cockles," Alton Cheney declared.

"Alton!" his wife scolded. "A gentleman doesn't say such things! What will people think?"

Gladys chortled. "They'll think your husband is correct, Agnes. If ladies had cockles, mine would be frozen, too."

Everyone laughed.

"We'll eat these cookies, Luke and I prepared, and I'll put the kettle on. Hot cider will warm your bones. You've got to save those voices. I'll add some honey to the pot."

The carolers streamed through the door, gratefully accepting the warm invitation. The citizens of Nevada had dearly missed Abigail Rose's generous hospitality. It had been seriously lacking in the last several months, but it now appeared she was feeling much better.

The cookies proved to be a delightful delicacy. Abigail pointed out that Luke had been a big help in their creation. Sweet, creamy frosting swirled on the tops of bells, trees, and animals, making them a heavenly treat for the eyes, as well as the stomach. Crispy around the edges and perfectly soft in the center, the golden morsels melted in your mouth. However, it was the cider, hot and aromatic, spiced with nutmeg, cloves, and cinnamon that rejuvenated the souls and voices of the merry band. Cup after cup was poured; until Abigail fretted she may have to make a pot of coffee to appease her guest's appetites.

But she was spared that task, as the clock chimed the hour, announcing the time for the carolers to gather up their things and start out once again. With the cookies nearly all consumed, and the cider reduced to an inch in the pot, everyone got up and prepared to leave, wrapping scarves around their heads and slipping their hands into fur lined gloves and mittens. There was the west side of town yet to reach, before they could call it a night.

"Thank you for your Christian hospitality, Abigail Rose," Hannah remarked, sincerely. "It's mighty good to see you feelin' more like your old self. I don't know how much longer I could have stood out there, in the cold. My eyes were startin' to freeze over." It was just that cold.

"Pardon us, Mrs. Donovan," one old brother interjected, "but Marvin and me noticed you ain't got yer tree yet. As it so happens, we got us one extra, this year. I told him I already done cut us one, but Marvin, he don't never listen to nobody. Stubborn as an old mule, he is. So, now we got us two. Nobody needs two Christmas trees!"

"Dammit, Cal, that just ain't so. I cut down my tree first, and you knowed it! You're just bein' quarrelsome."

"Am not."

"Are too. Don't you argue with me, Calvin. I'm the eldest and what I say...goes."

"You're the son of a mangy old polecat, Marvin. Even if'n you are my only brother."

The old man snickered. "Yep, I reckon I is...and what's worse...yer one, too!"

Both men broke out in great peals of laughter, completely forgetting their difference of opinion—as was often the case. They'd fight like wild coyotes, one minute, and the next they would be extolling each other's virtues.

"You can have our extra one, Abigail Rose. I'll bring it up, tomorrow," Marvin declared.

"I will," Calvin countered.

Marvin growled. "We both will, Miss Abigail. It's our gift to you."

Abigail was startled by the brother's generous offer, but not a bit pleased. A tree was an unnecessary reminder of what she most missed about the holidays. So far, she had been able to find pleasure with Luke, but a tree was simply too much. "Now, boys, I am truly grateful for your kind offer, but I don't intend to put up a tree, this year. You see, it is only Luke and myself, and we're not prepared. I don't even know where my decorations are. We'll be fine without one."

"Both men shook their heads. "No, ma'am," Calvin insisted. "Christmas just ain't the same without a tree. I'm sure the little tyke would like to have one."

Abigail turned her eyes to Luke. "Is that true, Luke? Do you want a tree?"

He smiled, but shrugged his shoulders, refusing to take sides.

"I'm sorry. It's very nice of you, boys, but we'll not be having a tree this year." It would be too much, too soon. Perhaps next year, she and Luke would put up the largest tree in all of Nevada... just not now.

Marvin tipped his hat. "Have it yer way, Abigail Rose. You always do. Thanks for the vittles."

"Always was a hard-headed gal," Calvin whispered to his brother, as they turned and followed their neighbors out the door. "Still real purdy, though."

◆ ◆ ◆

The dawn of December 22nd came early. As the bright light of morning cast its warm rays across her face, Abigail groaned aloud. She felt as if her eyes had been glued shut and sand had been poured down her throat. "Lord preserve us," she moaned, as she let her feet drop to the floor. She was exhausted, and there were so few days before Christmas in which to do all she had promised Luke. Where had she found the limitless energy to do what needed to be done, in years past? Patricia and her father always had some hare-brained notion to do something ridiculous; something that resulted in her having more to do. One year, she had been forced to stop decorating the parlor, in exchange for the opportunity to watch her family skate around on Abernathy's pond. Ignoring the warning signs of thin ice, they skated without fear... that is until the cracks began forming and snapping like gunshots, under their feet. With arms flailing, feet scrambling, and a few hard landings on their behinds, they managed to make it to shore before the entire surface crumbled into the freezing water, sinking to the bottom. There had never been any actual danger of drowning, as the pond was only four or five feet deep, but one could certainly catch his death, if he were to fall into the frigid water. After scolding them severely, Abigail dressed her family in warm flannel and soft woolies and gave them soothing beverages to drink, before ordering them off to bed. Only then, could she return to the work of hanging the greens.

After the frank observations of her friends, only the night before, Abigail began to feel slightly guilty in denying Luke a true expression of the holidays. This was perhaps his very first Christmas, and he deserved more than what she was giving him. True, she had wrapped a few gifts to be given out on Christmas morning, and they had had tremendous fun baking cookies, but the house still looked bleak and void of any real cheer; even to her. Perhaps if she put her mind to it, it would be possible to liven up the rooms with a smattering of red ribbons tied here and there, and some scented fruit to freshen the air. Maybe Luke would enjoy exploring the attic, with her. Surely, there would be something useful there; a bit of tinsel or a sheet of colored paper could be used to make the house more festive.

"Luke," Abigail said thoughtfully. "Are you afraid of spiders and mice?"

All color drained from the boy's solemn face, causing it to

take on the color of pale parchment, however, he shook his head in denial. That was all very good for him, Abigail thought to herself, but she was terrified of the creepy, crawling things. That was the reason she had ignored the attic for so many years—that and the fear of confronting old ghosts.

She took a deep breath and reached for his small hand. Pointing to the ceiling, Abigail announced, "We're going exploring, Luke...up there. I know there are some things we can use to fix this old house up, just in time for Christmas Eve. I'm looking for a spool of red ribbon and maybe I'll find several yards of unused lace. There are boxes galore. You're bound to find something useful. Are you willing to face the creatures that lurk in the attic?"

Luke swallowed and nodded his head. His eyes were enormous with trepidation, but he was on a mission, and he had only another two days to complete it. He wouldn't let any long-legged, hairy critter stand in his way. Besides, he didn't think they ate little boys.

"Fine," she stated. "Follow me."

Through the small door, at the back of the house, and up the enclosed stairwell, they climbed, keeping their eyes open for any spider or mouse that might lie waiting in their path. The dust was thick, but fortunately, the webs were few and far between, and could be avoided entirely, putting Abigail's fears at ease.

"Not so bad, I see," she declared, as she looked around the cramped quarters. Her eyes were immediately drawn to familiar items, things forgotten about or thought to be lost. "I'll go through these boxes, and you may go through the trunk. I don't expect you to find anything of much use, but one never knows. Look for anything that can be used to brighten up the parlor...an old piece of jewelry, perhaps," she offered.

Soon, the duo were waving away dust motes and wading through inches of time, left on the surface of discarded valuables —hats, gloves, shaving mirror and mustache cup. An old book with the cover barely attached, a pile of discarded papers, and a dented brass spittoon were stacked precariously, on a rickety, scarred table. Abigail quickly became engrossed in a box of crochet patterns; some she recognized as ones her mother had passed down to her. Luke had his head buried under the lid of a small trunk, having found nothing of interest in the larger one. Inside, hidden under layers of petticoats, he discovered a small box, tied securely with twine. Carefully, he worked at the knots and finally succeeding in slipping the lid off.

He remained quiet and still, continuing to sit there, staring at the strangely familiar likenesses. Photographs of Abigail Rose and a baby with yellow hair, smiled up at him. There was one of a tall man in a Confederate uniform, as well as one of a Union soldier. Within this little box, the story of this ladies' entire life could be told. Instinctively, he knew what power it possessed. Making a decision, and with his hands trembling, he replaced the lid and tucked the box safely under the petticoats, it precious contents to be preserved for a special occasion. Suddenly, a bright shiny object caught his eye, and he pulled out a row of red buttons from the trunk. He held them up in the air for approval.

"Those are beautiful, Luke," Abigail exclaimed. "I found some lovely green wool pieces. Together, we can cut and sew large holly leaves and berries, and hang them in the windows. They will look quite festive. And I've found my red ribbon...some white, too. We'll tie them around the chandelier. Won't we have fun?" she asked, her face beaming. "I think we have found what we were looking for. Let's leave this place for the mice and scurry on back, downstairs. I'll make some hot cocoa, and we'll get to work."

Luke smiled, and shut the lid to the small trunk. Stuffing the buttons in his pocket, he helped Abigail to the stairs, making certain to latch the door behind them.

Within minutes, they were seated at the kitchen table, with thread, needles, and scissors in front of them. Abigail sketched out the pattern of the large leaves, leaving the placement of the buttons, entirely up to Luke. "Which do you prefer...cutting leaves or sewing holly berries?"

Luke chewed on his bottom lip, trying to decide. Both were important tasks, and he was capable of doing either with great skill, but he decided to sew berries onto leaves, and reached for the needle and thread.

"Just as in nature, you can put them anywhere you like, only I do believe they occur in clumps," Abigail tactfully suggested.

It was then that Abigail noticed the thread. It was white, and that would never do. "Oh, no," she lamented. "That is going to stick out like a sore thumb. My mother would never have approved." Glancing up at the clock, on the wall, she stood and removed her apron. "I've got just enough time to run to the mercantile and buy some red and green thread. Will you be okay staying here, Luke? I'll be gone only a few minutes."

The boy nodded, as he carefully placed three red buttons on a piece of green fabric. He had much to do, and not a lot of time to get it all done.

"Very good," Abigail stated. "You sit here, drinking your cocoa. I'll be back before you can say, whippersnapper."

He chuckled, knowing it was impossible for him to say the funny word in any length of time.

◆ ◆ ◆

She didn't like leaving Luke at home alone, but he was busy working at the table and wasn't likely to get into any trouble, in the short time she would be gone. Keeping her head down, her eyes on the ground, and her nose buried in the warm fur collar of her coat, Abigail forged through the snow toward the store. Hopefully, the mercantile would not be sold out of red thread. Green could be substituted, but she really preferred red.

"Rosie?"

Abigail came to a sudden stop, at the sound of her name. Looking up, her eyes searched down the sidewalk and saw no one in front of her. Maybe it had been the sound of the wind calling her name, as it blustered down the street, snapping twigs and blowing debris into the alleys. Tugging firmly on her hat, pulling it down securely around her ears, she resumed her trek.

"Rosie! Is that you?"

The voice was louder this time, causing Abigail to nearly trip over her own feet, as her toe caught on a warped board. It couldn't have been a trick of the wind. "Who is calling me?" she hollered out.

A tall man jaunted across the road and stopped in front of her. His face was covered with an unruly beard and his curly red hair sprung out from beneath his hat. Laugh lines framed his brilliant green eyes. He reached for Abigail's hands.

"It is you," he gasped. His eyes filled with tears. "I never thought I'd see you again. I heard you were…I mean, I thought you had moved on after the fire and all."

Abigail's head was spinning. What was this stranger babbling about? What fire? And why would she have moved on? Without warning, her heart nearly leaped from her chest. Only one person had ever called her Rosie, and it couldn't be him. He had been killed on the Sultana.

"Joshua?" she heard herself ask, as if in a dream. It was impossible. Her head started to swim, as her knees began to buckle. She felt strong arms wrap around her and catch her as she spiraled to the ground. The next thing she knew, they were in the Sweet Shop, and a cup of warm tea was being brought to her lips.

"Take a sip, Rosie. It will warm you. I guess seein' me came as quite a shock, for ya."

There was that warm, masculine voice, again, and it was addressing her as Rosie. "You can't be Joshua," she murmured.

The man watched as she took a swallow of the aromatic tea. It tasted divine and calmed her nerves, clearing away much of the vagueness that had taken over her brain. Peering into his eyes, she discovered them to be strangely familiar. It just couldn't be, she told herself. Not after all these years…could her Joshua have truly returned to Nevada?

"You're dead," she murmured. "You were killed on the Sultana."

He snorted. "Almost was. I always was a good swimmer, Rosie. That horrible night, it saved my life for sure. But I don't want to talk about that now. How have you been, Abigail Rose? Have you been happy?"

Abigail could barely speak. Joshua was sitting at arm's length in front of her. He hadn't died on the steamship, after all. The most she could muster was a nod of the head. She had been happy. Patrick Donovan was a loving and supportive husband. Their daughter was all that a child could be. And now, she was a grandmother of two. Yes, until recently, she had been extremely happy. Life had been good. Now, she had Luke.

"I was gonna ask about ya, but I just got into town, only a few minutes ago. I ain't even got my room at the hotel, yet. I was haulin' some furniture up to Kansas City, from my place, when I broke an axel. This close to Christmas, it might take a couple a days to get her fixed." He grinned, his eyes squinting with pleasure. "It sure is nice to see ya, again. Yer as pretty as you ever was. I've thought about ya, over the years."

With the help of the tea, and sound of Joshua's wonderful words, Abigail found herself warmed through and through. A quiet peace was beginning to settle around her, leading her to believe everything in the world was beginning to right itself. There was an order to things, which was now only being fulfilled. "I've been quite happy, Joshua," she said, softly. "And I'm glad to see you again, too, only I can't see your dimple, hidden under all those whiskers. I have so many questions for you. Could you come to dinner? I live at the end of the street, just a few doors away. And I have the most charming little boy staying with me. I'd like for you to meet Luke."

Joshua raised a brow. "He's not your son?"

"Oh, no," she sighed. "I found him on my rear porch, practically frozen to death. Please say you'll come," she entreated.

"How can I refuse ya, Rosie? I'm certainly not gonna let ya go, not now that I've just found ya. When's dinner?"

"Be there at six," she said eagerly. "Right now, I have an errand to complete, and I must return to Luke. A boy can get into such mischief, if left unattended for too long." She stood and took his hand. "I still can't believe it is you…Joshua Benson, after all these years."

"Will I meet your husband this evening?" he asked.

"No. I'm a widow. I have been for a couple of years, now. My daughter, Patricia, is married and lives with her two babies in her husband's hometown of Richmond, Virginia. It is such a far piece to travel; I don't get to see her very often. Are...are you married?" she stammered.

He shook his head. "My Sharon is gone, too. She'd been sickly for some time. I'm all alone, now. We never had no children. That's my biggest regret. I would have liked to have left a piece of myself behind. It's good you've got yer daughter and grandchildren."

"Yes," Abigail quietly muttered. If Joshua only knew the pain of being forgotten by those you love, he might not feel so envious. "Thank you for the tea and your strong arm to lean upon," she said, as she slowly made her way to the door. "I can't tell you what it means to see you here, in Nevada. See you at six o'clock, sharp."

"Sure thing, Rosie."

◆ ◆ ◆

By the time Abigail reached home, she was floating on air. When had the world righted itself," she wondered? It seemed to all begin with the discovery of little Luke. Since he came into her life, she felt rejuvenated, eagerly anticipating the arrival of each new day. What a difference the little child had made in her life. It was in conceivable to her, that only a few days earlier, she had been intent on throwing away this precious gift of life. Luke had saved her.

Brushing off the snow, and stomping her feet, Abigail Rose called out. "I'm home, darling. I apologize for taking longer than I had expected, but I ran into an old friend...a very dear friend. He's coming to supper," she announced as she walked back toward the kitchen. Surprisingly, Luke wasn't sitting at the table, and the scraps of green wool were left untouched; the shiny red buttons were stacked in orderly rows, waiting to be sewn on the leaves. Where could he have gone?

"Luke? Where are you?" she hollered, making her way to his

bedroom, where she expected to find him sprawled out on his bed, sound asleep. But the room was empty. "Luke? Can you hear me calling you?" She glanced into her room, and saw only a chair out of place. She must have pulled it away from the wall, while dressing earlier in the day, and forgot to put it back. Snapping her fingers, Abigail knew just where to look.

Lifting the latch, she pulled open the odd-shaped door. "There you are! I've been calling for you. I suppose you couldn't hear me with the door shut. Patricia couldn't, either." Then she grinned. "At least that is what she always said. Have you found something to keep you busy?" The moment her eyes settled on Luke, she noticed his odd reaction, as he quickly tucked a wrapped bundle into a basket, behind his back. "What do you have there?" she inquired.

His eyes grew huge, as if he had been caught doing something he oughtn't. He shook his head and pretended to be interested in a small picture book.

Abigail wasn't fooled, but she also knew a child required a little privacy. "That's perfectly okay, Luke. You can do whatever you wish, under these stairs. It's your kingdom, after all. I wanted to let you know, I purchased the thread we need, but I'm afraid I don't have time to be sewing just now. I must be attending to our supper. You see…my very special friend, Mr. Joshua Benson, will be eating with us. I thought he was lost at war's end. The war was over, but he was on a steamboat, trying to get home, and it exploded, killing more than two thousand men. Can you imagine?"

Luke's eyes reflected the imagined horror of the moment, and quickly overflowed with tears. He felt the pain of others, intensely. Sensitive and loving, this child was uniquely wise.

Abigail saw what her words had done. "Oh, I'm sorry, Luke. I didn't mean to make you sad. I'm still trying to come to terms with his survival. It's a miracle. I hope you like him. He doesn't have any children of his own. Perhaps we…I mean, I hope you like him, too." It was greedy to expect them to be a family. She already had more than her share of blessings.

"You can play for as long as you wish, Luke. If you want to

leave our sewing for later, that will be acceptable. We have all day, tomorrow."

Luke nodded his head, grinning broadly. He hadn't quite finished his surprise.

"Very well," Abigail said. "I'll call you when it is time to get cleaned up."

Luke heard her light steps, as she walked from the stairs into the kitchen. He listened to her lovely voice, as she began to softly sing songs of the season, hymns they had sung only the night before. It was obvious; at long last, Abigail Rose was beginning to feel the true magic of Christmas. Reaching behind his back, he retrieved the hastily concealed bundle. Being exceedingly careful, he took each fragile photo out and placed it in a straight row, side by side, with the others. Some could benefit from a little cleaning, while others needed some kind of frame. Frames could be made of the things he had on hand.

As his fingers went to work, he chuckled to himself. Thankfully, Mr. Benson had appeared when he did and had kept Abigail Rose occupied, or he could have been caught snooping in her room. He preferred to think it was investigating a mystery, but it was snooping—undeniably—but for the best of reasons. The last time she had taken him into her room, he had noticed the corner of a bag, peeking out over the top edge of her wardrobe. It was mostly concealed by a piece of trim, with only one corner slightly visible to the eye. But his curiosity was peaked. What could possibly be wrapped in the oilcloth, tied with string, he wondered?

Glancing back over his shoulder, he pulled a chair away from the wall, carefully climbed upon it and, standing on wobbly toes, he reached up and gingerly removed the dust-covered object from its hiding place. It was soft and pliable, and covered with age. It was a hidden treasure, no doubt, and something very precious, but forgotten. The climb down from his perch, with the package tucked securely beneath his arms, proved to be trickier than he had imagined. For an instant, he almost lost his balance and was forced to jump to safety. As soon as he landed, he scurried off to the little room beneath the stairs, to have a better look. He knew he would have his privacy there. Even if Abigail Rose came home early, she wouldn't think of intruding into his private sanctum.

The knots were intricate, as if to discourage anyone from opening the package. But Luke was determined. This was an important discovery. He could feel it in his bones. As the cloth was turned back, it revealed something of such beauty, his hands trembled and he held his breath.

The colors were of the rainbow, and as bright and lustrous as the day they were sewn together. The workmanship was superb; tiny, regular stitches connected the scraps in a flowing pattern. Masterful embroidery created birds and exquisite flowers, and spelled out one particular name...Abigail Rose. It was a baby quilt...and it was Abigail's, sewn by her mother's own adept hands, no doubt from fabrics she had lovingly gleaned from her dresses, and her pa's everyday shirts. Lace, which she had crocheted in the wee hours of the morning, edged the entire quilt. It was breathtaking, indeed, and something utterly priceless. Why had it been relegated to collecting dust on top of a wardrobe? Someone should use it.

Luke let his small hands glide over the smooth cloth, admiring the soft tucks and the neat, padded squares under his fingertips, as he tried to figure out what should be done with it, when someone banged on the front door. It was not a polite knock, but a loud, rapid bang. He jumped up and ran for the door.

"There ya be, son," Calvin Stark growled, his whiskered face completely obscured by the soft, evergreen branches of a tree. "Stand back! This dagnabbit tree is heavier than it looks."

"Mayhap it's 'cause yer gittin' too old," his brother snickered. "Never was no stronger than a pup."

Calvin shoved the tree against the porch railing, and put up his fists. "You shut yer trap, onct and fer all, Marvin. I'm as strong as I ever was. If'n you weren't so all dern lazy, I wouldn't have to do everthin'."

"I done cut down the tree," Marvind argued. "It's sittin' in a bucket, just this minute. You're the one what cut this'n down, and we didn't even need it. Tis only fair that you have to do the heftin' of it."

Calvin wiped the sweat from his brow, with the back of his tattered glove. "I reckon so, but it's goin' fer a good cause. The least you could do is help me haul it into the house."

Marvin groaned, but bent to pick up the trunk. "Lead the way. Get outta the door, little feller," he shouted. "Make way."

Out of the blue, a brilliant idea came to Luke. He squared his small body in front of the entrance, planted his feet far apart, and placed his fists on his hips. He shook his head and pointed around to the back.

"You want we should carry this around to the back door?" Calvin whined.

Marvin dropped his end, creating a loud thunk, on the porch. "Now, see here, little man…this is a gift for Miss Abigail Rose, and we don't cotton to the idea of a little squirt like you, tellin' us where to put this tree. It's heavy, and we're bringin' it in through this here, door."

Luke frowned, and attempted to stare eye to eye with the stubborn, cantankerous old man, never allowing himself to blink. Again, he pointed around to the back of the house.

Suddenly, Marvin began to chuckle. "Well, I'll be a dirty bird. If you don't beat all, little feller. You standin' up to an old grizzly like me, shows ya got gumption, and I admire that." He turned toward his brother, "Pick up yer end, Calvin. Let's get this tree around back."

Calvin laughed. "I wouldn't have believed it," he said, winking at Luke, as they hoisted the tree up onto their shoulders. "Should we carry it through the kitchen?"

Luke smiled, but shook his head.

"Just leave it on the porch?"

The boy nodded. The porch was perfect.

As soon as the men deposited their offering on the rear porch, arguing as to which way to lean it, Luke rushed back to his private domain, beneath the stairs. The precious quilt awaited, and so did the box of irreplaceable pictures. Abigail would be returning soon, and he had to hurry.

Thankfully, she had been detained. He heard her the moment she came through the door, but he needed time to put things away, before coming out to face her. When she unexpectedly threw open the door, he was certain she would see the flashing colors of the baby quilt. It was a miracle she hadn't. He needed to be more careful, if he was going to surprise her.

As it turned out, it was a very busy day for both, Abigail and Luke, and just before six o'clock in the evening, she discovered Luke in the parlor, curled up in a chair, and snoring softly. She carried him off to bed and tucked him in, under the covers. When he was comfortable, she bent over and placed a kiss on the sleeping boy's forehead. "Thank you, child, for coming into my life when you did. I needed your companionship, and I've grown to love you, dearly," she whispered. "Sleep tight." And she turned to leave.

If she had tarried, but a minute more, Abigail Rose would have seen the faintest trace of a smile upon Luke's lips. Everything was nearly ready, and his heart rejoiced.

CHAPTER SIX

The mantle clocked chimed six, and a firm knock was heard at the door. He was right on time. Abigail removed her apron, placed it on the back of her chair, and then surprisingly, she ran to the door, feeling like a girl of seventeen again. Quite out of breath, she patted her hair, straightened her sleeves, and slowly opened the door.

"You're punctual, I see," she blurted.

Joshua chuckled at her unique greeting. "Have you forgotten? I was always prompt when it came to dinner."

Abigail laughed. "And, if I recall, you were always early when it came to picking me up in your pa's buggy."

He nodded. "That's because your father insisted you be home before dark. I had to have as much time with you as I could get. Now that I've explained my punctuality, may I come in, Rosie?"

"Mercy me!" she gasped. "I sometimes have the worst manners. Come in," she said, pulling on his arm. Spying a box tucked close to his side, she had to ask, "Is that candy in that box?"

"It is. Why do you ask?" he teased, as he removed his scarf and coat.

"Oh, no particular reason. I just thought maybe you had brought it for me."

"Bring you candy?" he cajoled. "Seems to me, you were never partial to chocolates."

"You're wrong, Joshua. I've always adored chocolates. You

must remember." Abigail could already imagine the soft, rich chocolate and creamy centers melting in her mouth. It had been years since she had celebrated anything with chocolates. It was one of the pure joys of life—eating chocolates.

Joshua pointed to a chair, and waited for Abigail's permission before taking a seat. He held the box of candy on his lap, in full view. Sniffing the chocolaty scent, he moaned with pleasure and rolled his eyes heavenward.

By this time, Abigail was practically drooling. "Stop it!" she snapped. "You're a horrible man, Joshua Benson. You know you brought those chocolate morsels for me. Do you want me to beg for one?"

He laughed and held the fancy foil box out to her. "No, darlin'. I don't want ya to beg. In fact, I want to give you everything you've ever wanted. I want to spoil ya with everything I have. Since we met this morning, my mind has been in a whirlwind. All I can figure, we've wasted too much time, as it is. You was married to a fine gentleman, and I had a good woman, whom I loved very much, but they're both gone…and you and me are here, together. I don't want to waste anymore time, Rosie."

Abigail's breath was taken away. Her hand froze. She was blissfully happy to see him again, but she never thought he would still feel this way about her. He did not know the woman she had become. She was not the same innocent young girl he had known before the war. Too much had happened. She had to make him understand that she had grown bitter and useless. Perhaps she would show him her derringer. Surely that would convince him to forget about her.

"Rosie? Say something. Do ya feel the same way I do?"

Abigail turned her back to Joshua. She could not say what needed to be said, if she had to look into his eyes. "I'm a different person, now," she began. "When last I saw you, my life was all planned out for me. We would marry, move to the next county, and start making our home. We'd have healthy, happy children, and I would visit with my ma and pa every other Sunday. We were going to be so happy—then you enlisted."

She spun back around to confront her old beau, with silent accusations shining brightly in her eyes. "Why, Joshua? You ruined everything! You destroyed what we had—what we could have had. That was the beginning."

"I thought—" he interjected.

She held up a hand to silence him. "And explain to me why it had to be the Union Army? I had to make one excuse after another for you, to everyone I knew. I got so tired of covering for you." She took several deep breaths, and then shook her head in dismay. "It made no difference in the long run, I suppose. My brother ran off and enlisted in the Confederate Army. Can you imagine if the two of you had come face to face? What would you have done, Joshua? Would you have killed Jeb?" She paused for a second. "You never came face to face, did you?"

Joshua sat silent, stunned by the passion of her argument, the forgotten box of chocolates balanced on his knees.

"Jeb died at Murfreesboro. Ma always dreamed of reclaiming his body. Pa promised to bring him home. You should have been here, when the militia burned down the entire town. Maybe it would have made a difference. Maybe my mama wouldn't have run back into the house and have the ceiling fall in on her. Then perhaps Pa wouldn't have taken off, seeking vengeance. They left me alone, Joshua!" she cried, tears running down her face. "I was seventeen and I had no one!"

The candy box crashed to the floor, as Joshua jumped to his feet and took Abigail Rose in his arms. He held her tight, so close she could hear the beating of his heart. He buried his face in her hair and kissed her over and over again, willing to let her cry it out. Everything she had said was true. He should have stayed behind and taken care of family. War had changed everything.

"My sweet, sweet Rosie," he whispered, his voice thick and hoarse with emotion. "What have I done to you? I beg you to forgive me, sweetheart. As I traipsed over this country, mile after wasted mile, my mind was always on you. There was never a minute when I didn't miss what I'd left behind. I can't explain why I enlisted in the Union Army, except I felt compelled to do the right thing. It wasn't just about slavery. I didn't want this nation to break apart. I loved this country and what it stood for. It's the place where I wanted to raise my family…with you, my wife. I didn't think how it would affect you and my folks. I was wrong, Rosie."

Abigail tried to catch her breath, and cease her sobbing. She had always despised showing weakness in front of others. That was something other people did, never her. "A woman lives for love, Joshua."

"Yes, and a man kills to protect it."

An uncomfortable silence followed, until Abigail gratefully accepted Joshua's handkerchief. She wiped her cheeks and blew her nose. "I suppose you're right. Glory be, I don't know what got into me," she sniffed. "Perhaps it is the excitement of seeing you again."

Joshua snorted. "If it was excitement that brought on those tears, I can only imagine how you'd react if I was to tell ya really great news."

She cuffed his shoulder. "Don't be smart, Joshua. I apologize for my sudden outburst. I've been cooking all afternoon; I'm worn out. I wanted you to enjoy your supper. Follow me into the kitchen where I've set the table. It's cozier in there…and don't forget my chocolates!"

He laughed. "Yes, ma'am."

Upon seeing the table set for company, two places placed across from one another, Joshua commented, "Looks like somebody is missing. Did the little boy already have his dinner, or did you warn him off?"

Abigail brought the ham to the table, putting it next to the mashed potatoes and carrots. The fragrance of clove floated up from the platter, as well as the scent of molasses from the glazed carrots. It was a very special meal and everything looked perfect. "Luke is sleeping, unfortunately. He may awaken, yet. I reckon the little guy has had a busy day. He's been trying to get ready for Christmas. I think he's working on a surprise, under the stairs."

Joshua's gaze surveyed the room. "I don't see much Christmas in here, or the parlor either," he stated. "Don't go in for that, Rosie?"

She blushed, as she poured the coffee. "I used to. My Patrick was as excited as a little child, when it came to Christmas. We hung evergreen in all the windows and above the doors. He taught our little girl how to make the most spectacular wreaths. They would go up into the woods and he'd shoot down enough mistletoe to hang all around the house, and still there would be plenty to share with our neighbors. I started sewin', knittin', and paintin' gifts and decorations, just as soon as the weather cooled. I may have had only one child, but Patrick and I saw to every person in town. Not one would be forgotten on Christmas. We did whatever we could. Christmas was a joyous time of year for all of us."

"What happened? What brought about this change?"

"There's no point to it, now," she said matter of factly.

"I don't believe you," Joshua countered. "Christmas is alive. You can't ignore it, Rosie. Are you havin' money problems? Is that it, and you're too proud to ask for help?"

"Ha!" she barked. "I wish that was my problem. There's no point to it, because there is no one to celebrate Christmas with. Don't you see? There is no one to admire a tree. No one to open a gift. I can't cook Christmas dinner for one person. I remember Christmases from so long ago, and it fills me with sadness. Everyone I have ever loved has left me. Once again, just like after the war, I am alone."

"You're not alone, Rosie. I'm here, now."

Abigail shook her head. "You won't stay; but I will be okay. Luke has come to live with me," she said smiling. Her voice grew light and her eyes sparkled. "I can't wait for the two of you to meet. I don't know what it is about him, but he gives me hope. I look into his silvery eyes and I feel comforted. It gives me such pleasure to be taking care of a child again. I feel useful. He'll have a Christmas, this year. It won't be anything fancy, but I promise, I'll make him happy. He deserves nothing less. Naturally, you'll spend Christmas Day with us."

Joshua reached across the table and grasped Abigail's hand.

"I would like that very much, Rosie. It's important that I meet Luke. I need to thank him for saving you for me."

Abigail swallowed a bite of ham, as she stared into Joshua's face. Could he possibly know what she had intended to do? Why else would he think Luke *saved* her? "I'm fine, now. Really, I am."

"I believe you." It was time for a change of subject, due to the peculiar way she was looking at him.

"I would have come lookin' for ya, after the war, but I heard ya got yourself hitched to a real nice fella. After bein' burned out, losin' your parents and all, I figured ya moved away and it weren't no use anyway."

She shrugged. "Patrick said he had admired me from afar. When word came you were on the Sultana at the time of the explosion, he figured I needed someone to lean on. He was very nice and so handsome. I think you would have liked my Patrick. We moved from Nevada for a short time, but it was our home, so when he could afford it, he bought us this house. I've loved it here."

Joshua cleared his throat. Of course, he was grateful Abigail had had someone to care for her, but he would be a liar to say he wasn't jealous of the many years that man had spent with her, in her life and in her bed. He was envious of the daughter they shared, and the grandchildren that crawled up onto his lap. Such pleasure, he would never know. "You were lucky, Rosie."

"What about you, Joshua? You were mighty lucky to have survived. You eventually got married, and by the looks of you, you've been prosperous in life."

"This ham is real good, Rosie. I see you became a fine cook." Snickering, he asked, "Do you remember that church picnic I took you to? You prepared a basket for me, all by your lonesome."

"How could I forget it? And it's not very gentlemanly of you to bring it up now, after all these years."

"Well, bein' poisoned nearly to death is a hard thing for a man to forget," he said grinning.

"How did I know custard pie would turn in the heat? My ma never mentioned it."

"Maybe, but it was no worse than the fried chicken. I don't

know which one made me the sickest! The doc thought I might actually die. You know, to this day I can't stomach custard pie."

"Yes, I recall all that, but I also remember you telling him that you ate some mushrooms you'd found in the woods."

"I didn't want you to be blamed, Rosie. I saw the regret in your beautiful eyes, and the sweet pout on your lips when I refused another slice of pie. I couldn't add to your embarrassment. It was a secret I was willin' to take to my grave. But I'll you here and now, a man couldn't possibly get sick from eating this fine meal, darlin'. I wager you kept your husband well satisfied." Realizing what he had just said aloud, Joshua could feel his ears turning bright red. Hopefully, she hadn't grasped the double meaning of his comment.

"I'll take that as a compliment, Joshua. Patrick never complained. Could your wife cook?"

Joshua grew serious. "Well, it wasn't her strong suit. Sharon, that was her name. Sharon Augusta Felecia Portland."

"That's sure a mouthful," Abigail stated. "Fancy, was she?"

He nodded. "Fancier than most gals around here, I reckon, but she was as sweet as they come." He grinned with mischief, staring at Abigail over his raised fork. "She was a sight sweeter than you was," he chuckled. "You sure had a way of vexing me. I never knew which thing to say or do."

"It kept you on your toes, Joshua Benson. For too long, you had the girls chasing after you. I vowed I wouldn't be one of 'em. You would have to chase me, if you were to have me." She paused thoughtfully. "It almost worked, but in the end, I cried many a night, wishing I'd been a little easier to catch."

Joshua put down his fork and got up, walked to her chair, and knelt beside her. With one finger, he gently stroked her cheek. "You were the one I always had my eye on. Them other girls were just to make you jealous. I wanted you to want me. I saved all the pay I received from the army, but when the boat blew up, that which didn't wash away became worthless bits of paper. I had saved it all for us, darlin'. You know that piece of bottomland, just east of the McIntyre place?"

She nodded, breathing soft and regular. These were the words she had prayed to hear for so long. She didn't dare say anything to spoil the moment.

"I had enough to buy it for us. That was goin' to be our home, Rosie...yours and mine. Tell me it's not too late for us, sweetheart. You and me, we've been given another chance. We've gone through so much. Don't you think we're owed a little happiness in our later years?"

Abigail looked away. She wanted to scream, *Yes! Yes! Oh, yes!* But was that just a foolish dream on her part? He had no idea how much she had changed over the years. It was more than just learning to cook. She didn't feel like the same person, anymore. She would eventually make him unhappy, and she couldn't abide hurting him. As much as she desired to be with him, she had no choice but to send him on his way and never see him again—for his own sake.

Abigail scooted back from the table, and walked stiffly to the sink, where she began to pump water in preparation of washing the dishes. With her back to Joshua, she gave him her answer. "What you say is very nice to hear, Joshua. It's been nice seein' you again, and reminiscing the past. However, we can never go back. You have changed," she declared. "So have I. I am not the same person you fell in love with, so many years ago. I dare say if we met today, for the very first time, you and I would barely be acquaintances. I am not biddable. I am not needy. I am neither charitable, forgiving, nor am I particularly joyous. Had it not been for Luke, I would not be celebrating Christmas in any fashion. Our union would serve only to make you miserable. It's best we part friends."

Within moments, Joshua was standing by her side. He grabbed her shoulders in vice-like grip, turned her around, and looked deep into her eyes. "What happened to you? Whatever it is, I can see you through it. Damn it! I love you, Abigail Rose, and I'll not take no for an answer. Explain yourself," he demanded.

"Fine! If you're so all-fired nosey, I'll show you!" she shouted, as she dried her hands on her skirt. "Follow me, but you must be quiet. I don't want to wake Luke. He'd be alarmed, and I won't have that."

They walked quietly to Abigail's bedroom. It was a pleasant room, smelling of roses and lavender. Nothing appeared out of place. Abigail walked over to her desk, and taking a small key from around her neck, she put it in the lock and opened the drawer.

"What?" she gasped, and began rifling through the clutter. "It's impossible! Where is it?"

"Where's what? What ya lookin' for?" Joshua had never seen her so flummoxed. Something was missing, and she was very upset. "If ya tell me what it is, maybe I can help you find it."

Abigail slammed the drawer shut. "It had to be him," she mumbled.

"Him? The kid?" Joshua asked.

"Luke, naturally. He's the only one that knew of its existence."

"What are we talkin' about here, Rosie? What's missing?"

"My pistol! My little pearl handled derringer is not in the drawer. It should be. I locked it in there, myself. Only Luke knew I had it."

Joshua plopped down at the foot of her bed. "Rosie!" he commanded, patting the space beside him. "Come here, and sit down. You're gonna tell me what this is all about, and you're not gonna leave out a thing. What on earth are you doin' with a pistol?"

Abigail's entire body began to tremble, and the tiny bit of food she had consumed was rising in the back of her throat. The gun was missing. Had Luke been playing with it? Should she wake him up? Had her foolishness placed him danger? Terrified she was going to be sick, she did as she was told, and quickly took her place next to Joshua.

Joshua waited for color to return to her face, before he pressed Abigail further. Her troubles ran deep, that was plain. "Rosie, my girl, explain how that innocent child knows you have a pistol."

She began to cry. "I'm ashamed. You'll never think good of me again."

"I'm not that easily chased off, Rosie. I have broad shoulders and a strong back. I can carry a heavy load. Now, tell me why you're so unhappy."

Abigail nodded, praying she would have the courage to unburden herself to this amazing man, and praying he would still be at her side, after her story was told. "After you left…after Jeb was killed and Ma and Pa passed on, I was half outta my mind. I was too young to know how to carry on. If it hadn't been for Patrick, I may have thrown myself into the river. It was that bad." She felt Joshua's strong grip gently squeeze her hand, giving her strength to continue. "From the moment we married, my life was almost ideal. We had our hardships, but nothing that no one else didn't have to face. There was never enough money. Work was scarce, but we got along. When Patricia was born, I considered my life to be almost perfect. Within a few years Patrick got a good job and we were able to buy this house. I was happier than any woman had the right to be…and I was totally dependent on my husband."

"Most women need a man, Rosie. That's just the way it is," he stated, softly.

"You don't fully understand. I needed Patrick for *everything*. I didn't know it then, of course. It was only after he died, that I discovered my entire bein' was mingled with his. Without him, I was nobody. I had no purpose in life. Maybe if my daughter and her children were living here, in Nevada, I might have found a reason to live; but without 'em, I just saw no advantage to it. I had a dear friend that I could talk to, but she had a stupid accident and died. Fell down a flight of steps." She snorted. "That was just like Libby. Never could walk at a stead pace. She'd run hither and yon, just like a child. Tripped over some damn stupid slippers she'd made." Abigail sniffed a few more times, dabbing at her red eyes. "That's why I had the derringer."

Joshua sat mute, his posture stiff and unyielding. He couldn't believe she was saying such asinine things. She was a good Christian woman and was loved by many people, himself included, and she was telling him she had thought and planned to commit the most heinous of all crimes. He had seen wounded comrades fall on the field of battle, begging to be put out of their pain, refusing to do it themselves, as it would be an affront to God. And here, was a woman willing to die because she was lonely.

"I discovered Luke shivering on my rear porch, the same night I was going to carry out my plan. I guess the Lord had other things in mind, as I couldn't turn my back on this poor child. He was dressed in rags and wouldn't have survived the night, without my immediate help. That was the beginning of a new life for me, I suppose. Luke needs me for everything, so I'm now the provider, and I like it very much. It was on that first night, he spied my gun, lying on the bed. It upset him and I locked it away—for good. I would have thrown it away, but I just hadn't gotten around to it. I've been busy baking Christmas cookies, Joshua. I've even gone out and bought a few gifts. I welcomed the carolers into my home. Love for Luke has changed my life."

"And now your pistol is missing," he growled.

"Yes. Should I wake Luke and ask him what he knows?"

"No, let the lad sleep. But in the morning, you have to find it, Abigail. Then I expect you to hand it over to me. Is that understood?"

She nodded, feeling as if she were a naughty child that had just been reprimanded. It was quite obvious Joshua was angry with her, and understandably so. "Now you see why I can't be with you? Surely, you're sickened by what I had planned to do."

Joshua got to his feet and began to pace. He said nothing, but mumbled softly to himself, as if the two halves of him were having an argument, one with the other. For several minutes, it seemed he was unaware of anyone else being in the room. Until suddenly, he stomped his foot loudly, and let out an enormous roar. He spun around, his eyes wild and fierce. "But ya didn't do it, Rosie. By thunder, ya chose to let yourself love and care for an innocent child, instead. I know all the losses you have suffered. I, too, have lost everyone important to me. Until recently, I thought I had lost the love of my life, but here you are, and here I am, and I'll be damned if I let your foolish notions stand between us. Deny it if ya must, but you are still the girl I fell ass end over teakettle for. You just need to see yourself through my eyes. What you were thinkin' of doin' is mighty bad, but the way I figure, it's between you and the Lord. I'll leave it at that. I'm not gonna judge ya, Rosie." He offered a hand. "Now let's leave this room—I can't breathe in here—and go back out and have some of that apple pie I smelled coolin' in the window. I'll pour the coffee and you can slice me up a big, healthy piece...not one of them dainty slices you women prefer. I feel like celebratin'."

Abigail rose as if in a daze, with a sweet, almost painful ache in her chest. Could it be truly over? Was it possible Joshua didn't despise her? It would take a few minutes to wrap her mind around it all, but she already felt lighter, knowing she was forgiven by the man she loved with all her heart.

CHAPTER SEVEN

Abigail could not remember sleeping better than she had the night before. After gazing into each other's eyes, for what seemed forever, over warm apple pie and hot coffee, she and Joshua had decided to spend this entire day together. He would get to know Luke and help them decorate the house for the holidays; find the perfect tree and pop some corn for the garland. They would make a grand day of it. She was actually humming to herself, when Luke joined her in the kitchen.

"Good morning, Luke," she chirped. "I'll have your oatmeal ready in a snap. Your bread is buttered and just waiting for the jam. Hot cocoa is comin' up."

The boy climbed up on a chair and proceeded to spread apricot preserves on his toasted bread, merrily licking the drips off his fingers.

"You've scrubbed your face and combed your hair without being reminded. It must be a special day, indeed," she laughed. "You sure are a fine looking young man. You're gonna grow up into a handsome man, someday."

Luke chuckled, and took a big bite of the toast. Today was the day he had been waiting for. Everything was ready. His purpose for being here had nearly been fulfilled. The sunshine warmed his skin, while the hot creamy oatmeal heated his insides. It promised to be a glorious day.

Abigail sat down across from Luke, perfectly content in watching him eat. He had a most healthy appetite, as long as it wasn't meat being served. He was partial to fruit and sweets, and would tolerate eggs, milk, and butter. Hopefully, she would be able to entice him into trying other things, in the future, when he was older. "I'm sorry you didn't get to meet my friend, Joshua Benson. He stayed for several hours after supper, but you slept through the night. It's important you get to know him, and like him, too. I think he may be in our lives from now on. He was my beau, a long time ago, back when I was a girl. We have been very fortunate to meet at this point in our lives. He's eager to meet you."

Luke wiped the hot cocoa from his upper lip, onto the cuff of his sleeve, and shrugged his shoulders with disinterest.

"Mr. Benson will be coming by, shortly. We're going to go shopping. After all, tomorrow is Christmas Eve. He thought it would be nice if he got us a tree…just a small one. I know you'll get on with him."

Luke shook his head intensely. It's not that he objected to meeting the man, but he didn't have the time. There was nothing he could do. His surprise was going to be ruined. He had no choice but to show Miss Abigail what was lying out on the back porch. Jumping down from his chair, he took her by the hand and led her out back.

"Gallopin' grasshoppers!" Abigail exclaimed, startled to see the small, spindly tree resting on its side. "That's a Christmas tree."

A brilliant smile filled his face, as Luke nodded in agreement, and tried to lift one end.

"Oh no, Luke. I'm afraid it's going to be much too heavy for either one of us to manage. It will have to wait for Mr. Benson. Did the Stark brothers have anything to do with this?"

The boy laughed, nodding again, and held up two fingers.

"Well, those sweet old fools…they just don't know when to take no for an answer. I suppose they swore you to secrecy. Were you going to surprise me with it?"

Luke covered his face with his hands and nodded, too embarrassed to be found out.

Abigail put her arms around the small boy and gave him a hug, enveloping him in her sweet scent of roses. "You're a good boy, Luke, and you did surprise me. I wasn't expecting a beautiful tree such as this. We'll have a grand old time decorating it. I'll have to go out and buy popcorn, cranberries, and whatever else I can find to fancy it up. Don't forget we have Gabe's stars to hang… one for you and one for me. I'm afraid we ate most of the cookies, but that is of little consequence. We'll have a real humdinger of a tree this year. You'll see."

The boy laughed and clapped his hands with excitement. She didn't know the half of it, he thought cheerfully. It was going to be the very best Christmas, either one of them ever had.

"We best be going in, child. The sun looks inviting, but I'm freezing out here, just the same. We're not dressed for this kind of weather," she remarked, looking down at her slippered feet and the hem of her robe dragging in the snow. "Joshua will be here in no time at all, and I'm not fit for company. You need to dress warm, too. We're going to make a day of it."

He certainly was.

By the time Joshua arrived at her door, Abigail was beside herself with worry. Luke was gone—missing. While she had been busy dressing, he had sneaked out of the house without letting her know his intentions. It was unlike him to be so thoughtless. However, the child did leave behind a drawing on the kitchen table, that of a little boy with curly, blonde hair, smiling cheerfully and holding a present in his hand. That was her only clue. Near hysterics, she pulled Joshua into the kitchen and pointed to picture.

"Yeah, sweetheart. It's a fine drawin'. The boy's got talent. Where is he? I'd like to finally meet him, else I'm gonna think he's just a bit of your fanciful imagination."

"That's just it!" she shrieked. "Luke's not here, and I have no idea where to search for him."

Joshua tried to make light of the situation, but he could see just how frantic Abigail truly was. She cared a great deal for this child. If he wasn't found soon, she would worry herself sick. "Now, calm down, Rosie. He can't have gone far. You get your coat, and we'll follow his tracks. We'll have him back home before you can spit. It's too cold out there to play for very long."

"I hope you're right, but I feel as if I may never see him again. I can't explain it, but there's something in that picture that makes me want to cry. I can't lose him now, Joshua. I need him."

It filled Joshua with sadness to see the way she clung to the child, thinking he was her salvation, of some kind. It wasn't good for her to be so devoted to a child that wasn't even her own kin. His ma could show up and fetch him back, any day now. "You don't need him, darlin'," he reminded her. "You're a strong woman and you will always have me. Don't go borrowin' trouble. We'll find him."

Pulling on her gloves, Abigail headed for the back door, where the little tree sat waiting for a man to bring it into the house. "Hurry, Joshua. I think I can see his footprints in the snow. He's heading away from town."

"I see 'em, darlin'. He's lookin' for something or someone, in particular. We'll follow him."

But they didn't find him. At one point, his tracks simply stopped and disappeared from sight. Perhaps the wind had blown through, filling his tiny prints with snow, but even Joshua had to admit it was puzzling. They continued on in the same general direction, but it was useless. They were freezing and no closer to finding the boy, than when they left the comfort of her house.

One glance at Abigail Rose, and Joshua knew the woman had no choice but to return home. Her cheeks were parchment white, and her lips were as blue as a robin's egg. "It's time to go back, Rosie," he declared, looking up at the sky. "There's more snow in them clouds, and I can feel the temperature droppin'. Before ya know it, we'll be caught out in a yuletide blizzard. You're near frostbit, now. We'll go back and wait for Luke at your house. He'll be needin' a warm stove and a hot meal, when he wanders in," he explained.

Abigail didn't want to give up their search, but she saw the wisdom in what Joshua was saying. Luke would definitely need to be warmed up. Not to mention, she could no longer feel her feet.

The last half mile, she felt as if she was trudging through the snow on two, wooden stumps. Her nose was numb and her teeth were frozen. It was time to turn around. "Okay, I agree with you," she mumbled half-heartedly.

Joshua couldn't believe she gave in so easily. "What? No arguin'? You must really be miserable, darlin'. I figured I'd have to throw ya over my shoulder, to get you to come along."

"No, I can see the truth in what you're saying, Joshua. Perhaps he's already home and waiting for his lunch." She perked up and her eyes grew bright again. "Maybe he's worried about us? Wouldn't that be funny, if all this time, he thought we had wandered away? Yes, Joshua, let's hurry. I just know Luke is waiting for us at home."

Abigail had found her second wind. Wooden stumps, or not, nothing could hold her back, as she raced back over their tracks toward home. Joshua found himself trying to keep up with her—and he thought she was fragile. He had been mistaken.

The tree was missing from the porch. "He's here!" she shouted. "Luke's home!"

The kitchen door banged, as she ran into the house, calling out the child's name. "Luke!" she yelled. "I'm back. Where have you been?" She waited for an answer. Receiving none, she repeated herself, as she made her way into the parlor. "Luke? Are you in here? Luke where are you?"

"Rosie," Joshua said, softly, "look over there, in the corner."

Abigail sucked in a breath. "It's the little tree. That's what Luke must have doing the entire time we were out searching for him. How in the world did he drag it in here? It weighs more than double his weight. And look here," she said, reaching out to caress a rearing horse cookie cutter. "He used the cookie cutters to decorate it. I think it looks very pretty."

Joshua put his arm around her shoulder. "There's a couple of tin stars on it, too."

"Those are the ones Gabe made. I told you about him. I wish I could have given Luke more. I think this might have been his first tree." Abigail could feel tears begin to fill her eyes. This little boy was so sweet and innocent, and it was obvious he had had very little in his life, in the way of extras. The least she could have done was to show him how to make paper chains, or pop some corn, or help him finish the holly leaves.

"Feelin' bad about yourself, again, Rosie?"

Could he read her mind? She sniffed and tried to stop the tears from overflowing. "I just thought that I could have helped him a little more. Wait til you meet him. He's such a darling boy. There's so much I want to do for him."

"You'll get your chance, sweetheart. For now, we need to find that kid. He might be asleep on his bed."

Abigail ran for his room. "I never thought of that!" Soon enough, she returned to the parlor, with tears running down her cheeks. She lost the battle to keep them in check. "He's not here… and," she took a deep breath. "His new clothes are folded at the foot of his bed. Even his fancy, red plaid shirt with the metal buttons. He wouldn't leave that behind. It is his favorite." She turned to Joshua with unanswered questions in her eyes, beseeching him for an answer. "I don't understand," she lamented. "Where has he gone?"

He folded her into his embrace. Speaking low, his tone strong and firm, he said, "I don't know, Rosie, but we'll find him. He may still come home, but if not, we'll learn where he went. Luke sounds like a might smart boy. He ain't likely to get himself into trouble, so ya don't have to worry about that. I'm sure everything is going to turn out fine. I'm going out again."

"No!" she protested. "I can't leave. I've already missed him once. I can't risk missing him again."

He kissed her forehead. "No, sweetheart. I don't figure on ya leavin' the house. You wait for Luke. Put some hot chocolate on the stove, bake some of his favorite cookies, and wait for him. I'm gonna go and ask around town. He should be an easy kid to spot. Someone's sure to know something. He couldn't have just disappeared. I'll come right back, just as quick as I learn something."

"As quick as I can spit?" she snickered.

"Quicker."

The moment the front door closed, Abigail threw off her coat, hat, and gloves, and made her way to the kitchen. In a flurry of activity, she dragged out mixing bowls, spoons, flour, sugar, nuts, everything she could possibly need. She had made up her mind to cook all of Luke's favorites. Naturally, they would have to be sweet and delicious, dripping with icing or covered in glaze.

*

"Rosie…I mean, Abigail Rose, is beside herself with worry. He slept in his bed last night, and she fed him his breakfast this mornin'. He even took her out onto the porch and showed her a Christmas tree he'd gotten from two old brothers."

"Them would be the Stark brothers. A little cantankerous, but good ol' boys, just the same," Alton Cheney explained. "I've only seen the little feller twice. Came in fer new duds. Strange little man, but I could see the powerful way Miss Abigail felt about him. He had the most unusual eyes. Sorry I can't help ya. This time of year, I'm too busy behind the counter to see what's goin' on out in the street."

Joshua smiled. He had heard the exact same thing all over town. It was the chaos of the season, he reasoned. Still, it was almost as if the child had just up and disappeared. "I sure hope the boy didn't run away on account of me."

The old man nodded, realizing the import of that statement. "Rosie, is it? Well, I'm happy for the two of you. That's a fine woman there, but she ain't a bit too happy, nowadays. It's a kind of melancholy, my missus says. Lots of women catch it, after their family moves on. A woman needs someone to care for. That little boy cheered her mightily, but it's a man's love I believe she really needs. Now don't go thinkin' I'm saying something I'm not sayin'. She doesn't have to have a man in her bed. What I'm tellin' you… she needs to know she's valued. I tell my wife every mornin' how much I depend on her to see me through the day. Then, at night, before I close my eyes, I tell her how much I love and need her in my life. Hell, I'd be in jail or worse, if it weren't for my wife. That woman took a no-account piece of manly flesh and made him into a decent human bein', respected and prosperous and with a chance to meet her again, on the other side of the Pearly Gates...instead of treadin' water in that lake o' fire. Miss Abigail Rose is much like my wife. A good woman who deserves more than what she's been given. Trust an old man. I don't think that little boy left on account of you. I think maybe he saw he wasn't needed anymore."

"That's an odd thing for you to say, Mr. Cheney," Joshua remarked. "Why would a little child think that away?"

"You said you ain't met him yet. Then you ain't seen his eyes. Maybe I'm just a fanciful old man, but I believe in miracles...especially at this time of year; and I'm tellin' you, that boy ain't from no where around these parts."

Joshua was beginning to feel the same way. There was something mighty peculiar happening, but he didn't know if he believed in Christmas miracles. He tipped his hat. "Thanks for your help, Mr. Cheney. I'll think on all you've said. I'm sure the boy will be found. Merry Christmas to you and your missus, and tell her I'm grateful for her words of wisdom."

Alton chuckled. "I'll tell her," he said. "And she'll agree with you. I was one lucky man when she asked me to marry up with her. Merry Christmas."

As Joshua was leaving the store, Gabe and his sister crossed the street, heading his way. "Hey, Mister," the boy called out. "Are you Mrs. Donovan's friend, the one lookin' fer Luke?"

Joshua stopped abruptly. "That would be me. Do you have some information?"

"Uh-huh. This mornin', 'bout an hour ago, Luke gave me these here gloves. They's brand new, and I didn't want to take 'em, but he wouldn't take 'em back. He gave my sister his new scarf."

The little girl rubbed her cheek against the soft, red wool. It was the prettiest thing she had ever owned, and she'd hate to have to return it.

"Where did you see him?" Joshua snapped.

Gabe's eyes widened, and he took a step back. "He was with a man and woman, sittin' up in a big shiny buggy. They was dressed real fine...rich 'uns, I reckon. He looked happy. They was all smilin'. Luke waved at me and somehow, I knew he was goin' home. He don't talk, none, but I knowed they was his folks. I heard you was lookin' fer him and I thought I should let you know."

Joshua put his hand in his pocket and pulled out a dollar. Giving the coin to the boy, he said, "You did the right thing, boy. I thank you for letting me know. Miss Abigail will be sad, but she will be relieved to know Luke is with his family. It was a matter of time, I suppose. You take this dollar and buy you and your sister something sweet. It's almost Christmas."

The smile on Gabe's face was worth five dollars. He'd not buy candy for himself or for his sister, but instead they would buy their mother a present for Christmas. He couldn't remember her ever getting one. This year would be different. "Thanks, Mister," he called out, running back across the street toward the mercantile. "Merry Christmas to you and Mrs. Donovan."

"Merry Christmas, boy," Joshua replied.

That was that. The mystery was solved. The little boy had no doubt either run away, or had been separated from his family. That can happen in a strange town or in a snowstorm. Thankfully, he'd found Abigail Rose to care for him until his folks located him. He'd be spending the holiday with his family. That had to make Abigail feel better. However, he regretted having to tell her Luke was gone.

CHAPTER EIGHT

"I can't believe he left without letting me know...and just before Christmas, too," Abigail sobbed, standing next to the tobacco shop. Her baking completed, she couldn't abide another minute confined in the house, pacing the floor, just waiting for news. "I had such wonderful plans. Do you think he'll be all right with that couple?"

Joshua put his arm around Abigail's quaking shoulders, and placed a kiss on the tip of her pink nose. "Yes, my darlin'. Somehow, I have the feeling he was glad to be goin' home. His pa looked like a nice man...although a mite peculiar, I was told. Gabe didn't speak to him, but George Ashby introduced himself. The man seemed cordial enough, accordin' to Ashby, but he said nary a word...much like his son, I reckon. I was told little Luke seemed right happy to see him, as he was lifted up into the buggy. They rode away, his little arm entwined around the woman's neck. George also stated she was quite a looker, if that helps."

"It doesn't," Abigail growled. "We don't even know which way they went." she argued.

"True enough. There's some confusion there. No one actually recalls seeing which way they went, but I reckon it don't make much difference, no how. Luke's in good hands, honey. That's what's important. He's back with family. You should be rejoicin'."

Abigail sniffled. "I don't feel like rejoicing. I was beginning to think we...Oh, never mind. I'm just a foolish old woman," she scolded. "It's all water under the bridge, now." Wiping her eyes, she attempted a deep cleansing breath, and turned her adoring eyes upon the big man standing with his arms wrapped tightly around her. "I found you," she sighed, "and that fills my heart with gladness. I'm going to miss Luke, terribly. Christmas won't be the same without him, but I'll have you to keep me warm, won't I? I can't ask for more." A sudden burst of winter air blew up the porch steps, lifting her heavy skirts, revealing her stockings. "Burrrr," she yelped. "Let's hurry home and warm ourselves up. I'm nearly frozen."

Joshua chuckled, knowing just how he would like to warm her up. "Shall I carry you, or do you want to make a run for it?"

Seeing the glint in his eye, Abigail took off across the road without saying another word.

"Hey! That's not fair," he laughed, as his long legs quickly made up the space between them. "I can see I'm gonna have to keep my eye on you. You haven't changed a bit, Rosie. Still just as tricky as when you were a girl."

"Why, Joshua Benson, I do believe that is the nicest thing you've ever said to me."

"Nicer than this?" he said softly, pressing his lips to each of her plump cheeks. For a few heavenly moments, it was as if they were the only two people on the face of the earth. They quite forgot they were standing at Abigail's gate, in full view of her friends and neighbors. The kissing didn't end until Joshua heard the snickering of small children, and the hushing of their mother.

Immediately, he jumped back, putting appropriate space between himself and Abigail. "Excuse me, ma'am," he blathered. "I—I—I mean we…"

"For heaven's sake, sir. Don't pay no mind to my little heathens. It's just nice to see two people in love." The woman turned her eyes toward her friend. "I can't say how nice it is to see you up and around again, Abigail. I was just by Virginia Settle's place, and you'll be happy to hear she's made it through the lung fever, and she's giving your care all the credit for saving her life. She swears if it hadn't been for you and your know how, she'd not live to see this Christmas. Ginny's weak, but doing much better now. You're a blessing, Abigail Rose…a true blessing."

"It was the Lord's doin'," Abigail responded. "I did very little."

"Well, nonetheless," the woman argued, "the whole community is lucky to have you. Now, you two lovebirds go on and finish what you started…although you might want to step inside," she giggled. "Merry Christmas, Abigail Rose," she called out, as she rushed to keep up with her feisty brood.

"Merry Christmas, Dorcas," Abigail replied. "Merry Christmas."

Joshua stood grinning. "*Dorcas*? She is one very intelligent woman."

"Yes, my love. Every first born female in her family shares that noble name." She snickered, slightly, trying hard not to laugh. "Not only is Dorcas one of my best friends, she also knows love when she sees it, and she's smart enough to realize we need our privacy."

"Not mention you're wearin' entirely too many clothes. We've got to get you inside the house, before you wilt from the heat."

"*What*?" Had the man lost his mind?

Joshua turned the doorknob and pulled Abigail inside. "I want to feel you in my arms, young lady, without the thick layers of wool and fur. I've waited too many years to dawdle now."

"Joshua!" she squealed. "You can't be serious."

"Can't I? I am as serious as a snakebite, darlin'. Get that coat off and toss it on the floor. I'll build up the fire and we can relax."

"Oh, Joshua," she purred.

The passing years dissolved into nothing, with the first, soul-tempting kiss. Luxuriating in front of the fire, lying upon the soft warmth of her coat, the two became wrapped in the rekindled glow of first love. A need as old as time, heated their blood, pounded in their heads, but common sense pulled them back. A shiver of unexpected pleasure ran up Abigail's spine, as Joshua's fingers moved along the slender curve of her back.

"It's as if you never aged a day, Rosie," he marveled. "You're as lithe and as lovely as you were at seventeen."

She moaned with desire, at his masculine touch. "Do I please you?"

His eyes feasted on the ripe fullness of her moist, swollen lips, as he cradled her face in his hands. "No one could please me as much. I've missed holding you in my arms, smelling your subtle fragrance. I can't pass a rose garden and not picture you in my mind, reaching out for me, offering me your lips. I stare into your eyes and I believe I'm offered a glimpse of heaven. Yes, Rosie, you most assuredly please me."

"Good," she quipped. Her taunting smile set his heart to pounding. She could feel it beating against her breast. His panting breath was not against her neck. "Come here and kiss me some more. I feel weak," she giggled.

She was so beautiful, so vulnerable, Joshua was afraid his heart was going to burst. Suddenly, they were back in each other's arms, his mouth devouring her sweet lips, his tongue searching for an entrance. She melted in his arms. Everything felt natural, so right.

For what must have been hours, Joshua and Abigail Rose clung to each other. When they finally pulled apart, Joshua found himself breathless and weak in the legs. Who would have thought his innocent Abigail could kiss with such abandon? He had half a mind to throw caution to the wind and toss all respectability out the window, and take her there, on the floor. There were, after all, limits to his control. But he knew he could never do that. Rosie was too important to him. He'd wait for her to tell him she wanted him in that way. Until then, he'd make a few trips out to the river and cool off.

"I gotta be goin', Rosie," he groaned, trying his best to extricate himself from her arms. "It's getting' late and folks might talk."

She slid an arm around his waist and tried to draw him near. "No, not yet," she protested. "Please stay a little longer. I'll fix you some coffee."

What he wanted couldn't be found in a cup. No, he really had to go. "Tomorrow's Christmas Eve, darlin'. I'll come early and help you finish the tree. I'm sure Luke meant for you to have a pretty tree."

"No," she pouted, sitting up, straightening her hair. "I like it the way it is. He decorated it, just fine. Besides, I don't have anything to put on it. I'll fix us some dinner and we can go to church. That will be nice enough. Maybe you could come back here and... well, would you consider kissing me once more? Your kisses are quite pleasurable."

Joshua laughed. "Yes, ma'am. I think I would be amenable to that. However, I can't guarantee I'm gonna stop with just one kiss."

"I won't hold you to one, Joshua. In fact...I really don't want you to leave now."

"It can't be helped, Rosie. If I stayed, I'd do something we'd both come to regret. That kinda thing ain't for folks such as you and me. I've waited a long time to have you, and I'm not gonna rush it now. Because I'm just a man, and a weak one at that, I have no choice but to go." He got to his feet, and offered his hand to help her up. "See me to the door?"

Abigail grumbled.

"I'll give you another kiss," he cajoled.

"Okay, I'll see you out, but you promise to be here early tomorrow morning. I'll fix breakfast."

"It's a deal. Now, come here and pucker up nice and purty."

Abigail approached him, and turned her face up to his, with the light of love shining brightly in her eyes. She pursed her lips and closed her eyes, waiting for her kiss.

Joshua couldn't help himself, nor could he keep his hands still. With his arms around her, his hands caressing her back, he nuzzled the side of Abigail's neck, causing her to fall into a fit of the giggles. Then he ran a smattering of tiny kisses up along her jaw to her chin. Finally, his mouth settled on hers, allowing him to once again, partake of their sweetness. Her lips parted with a breathy sigh of contentment. In that second, he knew she belonged to him.

"Sleep well, my love," he whispered.

"Thank you, Joshua," she muttered softly. "I know Luke is safe, but you made his absence much easier for me to bear."

"I'll always be here for you, if I can. Our destinies were meant to be entwined."

"That's lovely," she said.

He chuckled. "I read it somewhere. Now go to bed. Mornin' will be here before ya know it."

"I love you," she whispered.

"I love you, too, with all my heart, Rosie. Goodnight."

"Goodnight," she answered, just before she closed the door.

Joshua pulled his coat closed, and slipped his hands into his pockets. He had lied. He'd never read those words anywhere. They were straight from his heart, but he thought they might sound silly to a woman like Abigail. But silly or not, that's how he felt. He knew the first time he laid eyes on skinny, pigtailed Abigail Rose O'Connor; she would be the only girl for him. Even though life presented him with obstacles and difficulties, the thought of his Rosie had never completely left him. She married. He married, and he had loved his wife very much, but she wasn't Rosie. Now, God had given them another chance and he was happier than any man had the right to be. Looking up, he saw a bright star twinkling overhead, brighter than all the others, and said a silent prayer of thanksgiving.

◆ ◆ ◆

It was Christmas Eve, and as daybreak approached, the sun struggled valiantly to burn through the early morning clouds, but failed to heat the frigid air a single degree. However, Joshua did not notice the cold as it sliced through the bottoms of his bare feet. All night long, he had tossed and turned, punching his pillow and warring with the uncooperative blankets; willing the moon to give way to the sun. He couldn't clear the image of one delectable woman from his mind; one with the most desirable lips and the smoothest skin he had ever touched. She consumed his thoughts and filled his heart with yearning. He wondered if she too, had awakened during the night, calling out his name? The ecstasy of it all was almost too painful to endure. But hopefully, the sublime agony would be short lived, for tonight, right after church, he was going to ask Abigail Rose to be his wife. If all went according to plan, and she accepted his proposal, they would be married by New Years. Unfortunately, all was not perfect with his plan. He had no ring to give her. Praying the mercantile would have something suitable for the loveliest woman in the county, he forged ahead with the arrangements. It would be a surprise to her—and hopefully, a pleasant one.

Abigail had hardly slept a wink, and she feared it showed on her face. How did Joshua have the ability to fire her blood to the point of near boiling, when Patrick did not? Her husband and been a kind and considerate lover. She had never complained—not once—but now, she had to wonder. What was it about Joshua? Just the lightest touch and he set her flesh aflame. His tender words of love soothed her spirit and caused her soul to soar. Gazing into her mirror, she no longer saw an old woman, bereft of everyone she held dear. Peering back at her was a pleasant looking woman, of mature years. She had bright eyes, warm, the color of cinnamon, and her cheeks were smooth, peaches and cream, she had always been told. Her lips were full and slightly swollen from Joshua's kisses. As she coiled her long hair into a neat coronet, pinned high upon her head, she reveled in the weight of the silky, thick tresses. Although there was a sprinkling of silver, shot through the lustrous auburn strands, her hair was still her best feature. Joshua loved to bury his face in it, sniffing its clean, floral fragrance. Smoothing her shirtwaist, and looking up and down at her image in the glass, Abigail grinned. All in all, she thought she was still rather pretty, but what most thrilled her was the fact her waist was still narrow and her breasts, although small, but still firm. Time had been kind to her and she was well pleased. *But why hadn't she seen it before? Was she now seeing herself through Joshua's eyes? What kind of magic was at work?*

The knock came early, just after sunrise. Abigail had to rush the last of her toilet. In her heart, she knew it was Joshua. Obviously, he had had problems sleeping, too, and that knowledge thrilled her. "I'm coming," she called out, glancing one last time into the mirror. She tucked a piece of holly into the coronet, and made her way to the door. She felt unusually festive.

"Good morning, Joshua," she greeted pleasantly, just before he plowed through the open door, practically knocking her off her feet. "My word," she gasped, startled at his unexpected behavior. "Whatever—"

Her words were cut off, as Joshua threw his long arms around her, pulling her close, and smothering her face with hot, passionate kisses. If he had been forced to wait, even one minute longer, he reckoned he would have surely perished. Kissing Abigail was like a drink of cool water to a dying man. How had he survived so many years without her? Now that he sampled her sweetness, he'd never be able to go on alone.

"Joshua," she managed to mumble, between his lips.

"Rosie," he sighed, as he took her lips again, running his tongue over their lush, soft surface. "Good mornin'," he finally replied, nuzzling her neck and nibbling her ear.

She began to laugh. "Good gracious. Can you at least allow me to close the door?"

"Dorcas isn't outside," he chuckled. "I looked, but I'll shut the door. Wouldn't want to lose any of this heat." His eyes danced with mischief. "I see you slept well."

"Yes. As a matter of fact, I did. Did you?" she taunted.

"Sure, I did. There ain't nothin' to lose sleep about."

"Liar," she giggled. "I didn't sleep a wink and neither did you."

"You mean to tell me, you were up thinkin' about me…all night? Knowin' something like that could go to a man's head, darlin'."

"Well, you're safe, I figure. There's not room enough in your head for any more compliments. I figure your head is about as big as it can get."

Joshua practically choked with laughter. "Come here, Rosie. Let me show you why my head is so big."

She wriggled free of his arms. "Before breakfast?" she yelped. "I think not, sir. I'm a proper lady, and I will feed you first...then I may let you ravish me...within proper limits, of course."

"Of course," he snickered. "Lead the way, my proper lady. I've got a hunger that needs satisfyin'...and it ain't for eggs. But if I have to eat breakfast in order to get what I want, so be it. I'll eat a whole wagon full of vitals, if ya ask me to. Don't let it ever be said that Joshua Benson ain't a gentleman."

Abigail took his arm and led him toward the kitchen. "I would never say such a thing," she teased. "However, it is rather early, I'm afraid. None of the fires have been lit. Could you see your way to—"

"Don't have to ask, darlin'. I'll have this kitchen goin' in no time. What we havin?"

"I thought you weren't hungry for food," she retorted.

Joshua was bent low, over the stove, lighting the kindling. Shutting the grate, he turned and looked deep into Abigail's flirtatious eyes. "It's time you were made aware of the kind of man you're fixin' to spend the rest of your life with, Miss Abigail Rose. I am a lusty man. I have a large appetite for good food, fine horses and strong cattle. But most of all, I have a constant hunger for one woman in particular...and I'm afraid I'll never get my fill. You are warned, Miss Abigail Rose. I'll never lose my appetite for you."

Abigail put down the spoon and mixing bowl. In three steps, she was in his arms, feeling his heart beat in constant rhythm with hers. It was heavenly, being held so close to the man she had loved all her life. Life was perfect, or it would be if she could see her daughter and precious grandchildren. Perhaps Joshua would take her for a visit, in the spring. He was a good, compassionate man, and he would surely not object.

"I'll never get the flapjacks ready, if we stand here, kissing all day," she stated. "I have a lot of cooking to do. It's Christmas Eve, remember?"

He sighed and reluctantly released her from his embrace. "I do. Put me to work, Rosie. I'll help ya in any way I can. I want this to be a Christmas Eve you'll always remember."

She giggled. "Well, I'd say you've started off in grand fashion. I don't see how I can ever forget last evening, or this morning's greeting. You are unforgettable, Joshua."

"That my plan, Rosie. Now, what would ya have me do?"

◆ ◆ ◆

The ham was in the oven; the potatoes, yams, and green beans were ready to be heated. The bread had risen beautifully, and the pies were sitting on the windowsill cooling, just at they should. Everything had proceeded smoothly, with no unfortunate surprises.

"You've fixed enough food here, to feed half the town, Rosie," Joshua remarked, seeing the table and sideboard, filled to overflowing.

"It's a bad habit, I suppose," she lamented. "I still cook for a family and friends. I plan to take a large portion over to Gabe's ma. Then there's always the Stark brothers. They pretend they don't need it, but when I leave, they are always wearing big smiles. None of this will go to waste."

"You're a good woman, Rosie. You may not know it, but this town relies on you. From what I've heard, Mrs. Abigail Donovan has been generous to a fault with her time and her goods. You chose to shoulder your heartache, alone. You weren't willin' to share it with your friends and neighbors. They would have helped lift you, darlin'. There's no shame in bein' lonely. We all need a hand, now and then. And it would have given them a way to help pay you back for all you've done for them. Never deny someone the pleasure of helping you."

Abigail nodded. For so long, she had been the one to come to the aid of someone in need. When she fell on desperate times, she was simply too embarrassed to admit she needed help. That was one mistake she'd never make again. It almost cost her her life. "I have many good friends," she admitted. "They all asked about me. I kept it to myself. It was selfish…I can see that now. We all need each other. The Lord planned it that way. It took a little boy to help me see it."

"I know you miss him, darlin', but I'm certain Luke is where he's supposed to be. You were just holdin' him for his folks. And the way I see it, he was keepin' you for me. It all worked out in the end. Don't you figure?"

Abigail smiled, and laid her head on his shoulder. "I figure you've got it right. I do miss Luke, but I never truly thought he'd stay. I was hoping he'd be here for Christmas, but I suppose it worked out for the best. I do wish I could have given him a beautiful tree. As it is, he tried his best." She sighed, looking at the little tree, its branches hanging low, the cookie cutters tied here and there. Thankfully, the two tin stars sparkled in the late afternoon light, adding some life and holiday cheer to the corner of the room.

"You know, Rosie," Joshua began, "I can't be stayin' in Nevada forever. I've got to get my axel fixed and finish my run to Kansas City. Than I have to return home."

"Where is home, exactly?" she inquired. She hadn't given much thought to his leaving. Avoidance seemed to be the best tactic.

"I've got myself a ranch near Neosho, down close to Springfield. It's one of the biggest in the state. You can see forever, over the hills and hollers. It has sweet water. Good open cattle country, too, and you should see my horses. Rosie, there ain't none to compare with 'em."

She could hear the pride in Joshua's voice, as he spoke of his beloved ranch.

"My wife never took to the land. She was a city gal, and the open spaces made her feel disquieted. Sharon tried, but when no babies arrived, she sort of gave up and lost heart. She did her wifely duties, as she called it, but I could see she was disappointed. That hurt me, because I always intended to do right by her. Then, a few years back, she lost her health. I got angry, because I thought she could have fought harder, but I believe she just gave up; preferring death to life with me."

"Oh, no, Joshua," Abigail assured. "You are mistaken. I am

certain she tried to live. No woman would choose death."

His green eyes suddenly sharpened, casting silent accusations her way. "You nearly did," he growled.

"I—I didn't know what else to do," she stammered.

"But you thought about it. You chose to take your own life."

Abigail countered. "You said we'd say no more about it. You broke your word. Do you wish to argue on Christmas Eve? You'll be leaving soon, and I don't want our last words to be harsh and unforgiving."

Joshua looked down at the floor. "You're right, Rosie. Forgive me. I spoke outta turn. I suppose there's a part of me that still grieves for the loss of my wife, especially when it seemed preventable at the time. Then I think about you, darlin', and what I almost lost forever..." Sniffing, he wiped his nose with the back of sleeve. "I don't know how we got around to this kinda talk. It wasn't the way I planned for this evenin' to go," he declared. "We should be celebratin'. We've got another chance at happiness."

Choosing to clear the air, Abigail changed the subject. "Tell me why you never searched me out," she demanded to know. "I have lived in Nevada for most of my life. I wasn't difficult to find."

He shrugged his massive shoulders. "I heard you got yourself hitched, so I figured there was no use in comin' back here. Plain and simple; I didn't want to cause ya any trouble. Besides, I don't know if my heart could have stood seein' ya with another man. I never lost track of ya, though. My sister, Louise, is a friend of your attorney's sister," he blushed, realizing he had just confessed to keeping note of a married woman. "Mr. John Douglas shared your most recent misfortunes, with her. I learned of your husband's passin'. You have my sympathies, Rosie. I know what it's like to lose a spouse, but you are still blessed. You can take consolation in your daughter and your grandchildren."

She smiled. "Yes, I am. However, we are not as close as I'd wish us to be. I'm afraid my grandbabies don't even know my face. I send them gifts, but it's not the same. My son-in-law is a busy man and doesn't have time for silly old women. His mother passed on, years ago. But I pray things will change."

Joshua took Abigail's hand. "I pray things will change too, my darlin'. I pray you will make my life complete."

"How do you mean?" she asked, hoping he would ask her to share his life with him.

"Rosie," he said, his voice sounding hoarse to his ear. He tried to clear his throat. "Rosie, I've been thinkin. I planned to ask you tonight, but—"

A loud racket suddenly sounded on the front porch, interrupting Joshua's train of thought. Before he could get to his feet, a sharp rapping announced visitors at their door. Without an invitation, the door suddenly blew open and a lovely woman, carrying an infant in one arm, and holding the hand of a little boy of about four years, with the other, stepped in, "Grandma!" the child squealed, reaching out for Abigail.

The room began to sway, and spots formed in front of Abigail's eyes, as her legs turned to jelly, refusing to hold up her weight.

"Mama!" Patricia hollered out. "We've surprised you. We've come for Christmas!"

"Mother Donovan," the tall man, encumbered with packages, called out. "We're all here, and with good news to share. You may tell your mother, Patricia," he urged, setting wrapped packages under the little tree.

"Not now, darling," she responded. "Mama is clearly overwhelmed. We should have written, but it was at the last minute, before we knew anything. There just wasn't time, I'm afraid. Would you like to meet your Rosie, Mama?"

Quite speechless, Abigail held out her arms. She was still in a state of complete and utter shock. Thankfully, Joshua had gotten his bearings and was taking coats and bags. Her daughter placed the sleeping child in her arms, as Connor crawled up beside his Grandma. He placed his chubby hand against her cheek and smiled. "My Grandma," he giggled.

"He looks up at your portrait every night before he goes to sleep. He knows you, Mama. It was important to us that you continue to be a part of our family, even though you lived so many miles away. Are you happy to see us?"

"I'm beyond words," Abigail managed to say. "I don't understand..."

"It's quite simple," Patricia chirped. "Murphy has been promoted." Her eyes trailed lovingly over her handsome husband. "I'm so proud of him. The company recognized his brilliance, and then they apologized as they informed him he would be required to move." She grinned. "That's the best part, Mama. We will be living in Kansas City. It's so much closer than Richmond. We can travel back and forth, several times a year. Or you can come and stay with us, if you prefer. We'll have plenty of room. We've rented an enormous house."

Joshua stepped up and placed a possessive hand on Abigail's shoulder. "I might have something to say about that," he said, grinning directly at the pretty young woman.

"Mama? I believe introductions are necessary."

"Forgive me, Patricia, but I am a little distracted just now. This baby is too adorable, and I have the most wonderful grandson. Just look at the two of them," she gushed.

Her daughter laughed. "Then I suppose I will have to acquaint myself. Would you care to enlighten me, sir? Just who are you and what do you mean to my mother?"

Joshua took no offense at her polite prying. She would soon be a part of his family—hopefully, and he needed to inform her of that fact. "My name is Joshua Benson. I knew your mother many years ago, before the war."

Patricia's eyes widened in recognition. "Oh, you're *that* Joshua Benson. I've heard about you. You were Mama's beau, that is until you ran off with the Union troops to fight against your own kin."

"Patricia!" her mother admonished. "You keep a civil tongue in your head."

"Relax, Mama. I don't mind that you were once in love with a Yankee. It's Papa, you married. However, I must admit...Mr. Benson is a very handsome man."

Abigail felt her face go scarlet. What had gotten into her precious daughter? "Patricia, you are embarrassing me," she scolded. "Mr. Benson was coming through town, on his way to Kansas City, when he had trouble with his wagon. As soon as it's repaired, he is traveling on. I don't believe he was aware I still lived here, until we ran into each other on the street. I don't know what you've imagined, but I can assure you…"

"Oh, Mama," Patricia declared. "I imagine he will make you very happy. I can see it on your face and in his eyes. I'm thrilled for you. You've been alone, far too long. By the sound of your letters, I was beginning to fret about your sanity."

Abigail shared a quick glance with Joshua. There was no way her daughter could have suspected her mental state. She had taken great pains to write cheerful letters.

The baby began to squirm. "Let me have little Isabella Rose. She needs to be changed. Is my old room still available?"

"It is now," Abigail answered. "You might notice a slight change in décor, but it is still your room. I think you might want to take Connor with you, dear. It seems the excitement of seeing his Grandma has put the child to sleep," she chuckled.

Murphy came forward. "I'll take him, Abigail. The little man's had a long journey. He'll probably sleep through to Christmas morning."

"You won't be going to church?" she asked, surprised that anyone would stay home.

"If Patricia wants to, then of course. Although, we might have to cater to two very cranky children."

Abigail laughed. "That would be my biggest pleasure. It would make my Christmas Eve complete."

Murphy nodded, as he lifted Connor into his arms. "We'll give him as much sleep as possible, and then we'll happily follow you to church."

As soon as he was out of sight, Abigail turned to Joshua. Happiness radiated from her. "Do you believe it, Joshua? My daughter and her entire family, here, in my house for Christmas. It's almost like old times…except for the tree. I don't believe I could be any happier."

"Not even if I was to ask you to be my wife before the end of the year?"

Abigail took in a deep breath. He had said the words. Joshua had asked her to be his wife. So much was happening, and so quickly, she couldn't quite grasp it all. She loved him, and she loved her daughter and grandchildren. She had been invited to come and live with them. She'd see the children grow up. Perhaps there would be more babies. Patricia would surely need her mother. Joshua would be fine on his beautiful ranch, with his cattle and his beloved horses. He had much to be proud of. He didn't need her...but oh how she needed him.

"Only that, would make me happier," she said, with a smile stretching from ear to ear. "I'm getting the better bargain, but if you're sure that's what you want...who am I to object?"

Joshua bent over and lifted Abigail into his arms. With her arms wrapped securely around his neck, he kissed her soundly. "I know exactly what I want, Rosie. I've always known. If you're willin', we'll be married by the end of the week. I'm sorry I don't have a ring, but I promise to buy ya a real humdinger when I get to Kansas City."

"I don't need a ring, Joshua. Right now, I have everything any woman could want. But I would like another kiss," she hinted.

"You're the boss, little lady," he chuckled, right before his lips found hers.

◆ ◆ ◆

The stars were bright overhead, not a cloud was present to dim their sparkle. It was the perfect December sky. Children sang of good tidings, as they strolled up and down the snow-covered walks, for the last time this year; their innocent voices blending perfectly under the starry sky. Enormous white flakes floated silently to the ground, shimmering under the light of the moon. It was a silent night, a glorious night to worship the birth of the Christ child.

Abigail took notice of even the smallest thing. The way the

air smelled clean and new, and froze her lungs has she breathed deeply. Her grandson, Connor held tightly to her hand, occasionally looking up into her face, as if he was reassuring himself, she was there. She saw the way Murphy gazed lovingly at her daughter. She carried Isabella Rose, while he kept his arm locked on her back, guiding and protecting her from whatever might come their way. The sound of the carolers, the ringing of sleigh bells, the greetings called out from one neighbor to another…she noticed it all. How could she have been so blind to the goodness and blessings in life? She didn't know what God had planned for her life. No one knew what the future would bring. As it turned out, it would have been a travesty to miss this Christmas. She had selfishly chosen a permanent solution to a temporary state of mind. This was the true spirit of the season. Luke, Patricia, the babies, and most of all…Joshua, had filled her life with immeasurable joy.

The snow crunched under their feet, as the Laughlin, Donovan, Benson party approached the steps to the white church at the end of the street. It's bell in the steeple, hung silent now, but would soon peal out announcing the news, right at the stroke of midnight—Christmas morn.

Men tipped their hats, while women gave small hugs. "Nice to see you, Abigail Rose," they would say. "Merry Christmas," was repeated again and again. Before they could take their seats, Abigail saw Hanna rapidly making her way toward them. An invisible cloud of gardenias preceded her.

"It's so good to see your family tonight," her good friend exclaimed, taking a quick appraisal of Joshua. "I thought you said they weren't coming this year? I know you were feeling a little blue, but things look as if they have worked out very nicely, after all. I'm happy for you, Abigail Rose," she said, her eyes beginning to tear. "You're my best friend, and I don't know what I'd do without you. I can be a silly old woman at times, but you seem to put up with me. For that, I'm truly thankful. Merry Christmas to you and your family, Abigail. You're coming to my house for New Year's Eve. I won't take no for an answer."

Joshua discreetly nudged Abigail from behind. She'd be on

her honeymoon, with him. That was one New Year's Eve gathering where she would be absent. He leaned in and whispered, "Let's sit down, before the rest of your admirers come our way. The baby is getting heavy, and Connor is asleep on his feet."

Abigail looked over, and sure enough, her grandson was teetering on his little feet, his eyes barely focusing. "That's a fine suggestion," she said, choosing the last row of pews for her family.

The pastor was eloquent. Christmas sermons were his favorite. The little choir sang cherished hymns, while the organist accompanied them. Smiles were one everyone's lips. The children were on their very best behavior, and sly looks were exchanged between parents. It hadn't changed much, over the years. The story was always the same. Joseph and Mary, riding on a donkey, went into Bethlehem, the town of Joseph's birth, to pay taxes. She was great with child, and there was no place for her to rest. It had been a long and arduous journey. The time came for her child to be born. They were allowed to take rest in a stable. There amongst the animals, delivered on a bed of straw, our savior was born.

Just Abigail knew it would, at precisely midnight, the big bell in the tower began to ring out the good news. Glad tidings of great joy to all who hear the word of God.

Joshua gave Abigail a proper kiss on the cheek, while Murphy kissed his beautiful wife, full on the mouth. "Merry Christmas!" everyone exclaimed in unison. It was Christmas Day.

CHAPTER NINE

"Oh, Joshua," Abigail sighed, on the short walk home. "Wasn't everything just perfect? I have the nicest friends and the most perfect neighbors. And you and Patricia and the children are so..."

"Don't say it, darlin'. We're all perfect," he laughed.

"Oh, you," she said, swatting his arm. "I mean what I say. I have the best family any woman could dare wish for. Just look at them," she remarked. "Have you ever seen anything lovelier than my family?"

Joshua paused, and took her into his arms. "As a matter of fact, I have. You are by far the loveliest creature I have ever laid eyes upon, Abigail Rose. And as soon as you are my wife, I intend to prove it to you every day."

"You say the nicest things."

The golden light shining through the parlor window, cast it's festive glow across the porch and down the walk, welcoming them home. "Did you leave a lamp burnin', darlin'?" Joshua asked.

Abigail shook her head. "I don't believe so. Did you, Patricia?"

Her daughter shook her head. "Maybe Murphy did. He's considerate that way."

He shook his head. "Not me, sweetheart. Do you think someone has been in the house?"

"Perhaps it was Luke," Abigail suggested hopefully. "You don't suppose he's come back."

Joshua released his hold on Abigail, handing her off to her son-in-law. "Keep her here, while I take a look see." He quietly stepped up on the porch and turned the door handle. It was never locked. He was not prepared for what greeted him. "Gallopin' grasshoppers! You've got to see this, Rosie" he gasped.

"Oh, my stars!" she shrieked. "Look at the tree!"

"What in the world?" Patricia muttered, as she sidled up alongside her mother. Only a few hours before, the puny little tree had been standing nearly bare. A few cookies were ready for hanging, and some ribbon was stuffed in a basket—but this was surely a miracle. "Who did this?"

"It had to have been Luke," Abigail whispered. "That's the only explanation." But when had he found the time or the materials necessary to complete the glorious transformation? He was just a little boy.

The family drew closer to inspect the many magnificent decorations bedecking the stately tree. Small photographs of loved ones were tucked neatly between the branches. Abigail's father, wearing his Sunday-go-to-meeting clothes, stood proudly behind her smiling mother, wearing her new Easter bonnet. In another photo, her tall, proud brother stood looking squarely into the camera, with his shiny brass buttons reflecting light. It was taken shortly before he left for the war. There was a miniature of her as a schoolgirl, as well as one of Betsy. Various images of Joshua and Patrick and Patricia, also hung on that lovely tree. Some of the photos were held in silver frames, while others hung from ribbons. What marvelous memories those pictures stirred. They had been "lost" for years.

"The tree is so beautiful this year, Mama," Patricia exclaimed. "You're very clever about keeping secrets. I had no idea we were going to come home to this."

"I hadn't exactly planned it, myself," her mother muttered, confused by what her own eyes showed her to be true.

"Where did you find all the old photographs? I thought they burned. Is that my Uncle Jeb? He was so handsome."

Connor ran to the tree, cupping Clementine in his chubby

fingers. "Baby Jesus," he squealed.

"I can't believe it," Patricia gasped. "It's my crèche. Wherever did you find it? I thought it was lost forever."

Abigail was stunned. "I—I thought it must have been tossed out long ago. I honestly don't know where it came from." Could Luke have found it and not informed her of his discovery? He must have. It was the only explanation.

"Clementine looks just the way I remember her...perhaps better. I thought I broke her tail. Papa did such fine work."

"That's because he was doing it for his daughter. You were everything to him, Patricia. He loved you very much and was always so proud of you. I wish he could see little Connor and Isabella now."

Joshua stepped up behind the women, his voice soft and gentle. "I believe he can, ladies. Can't you feel his presence all around you, filling this house with love?"

The women exchanged wondrous looks. The house was warm and overflowing with a sense of peace and love for one another. Their hearts were filled with precious memories—enough to last a lifetime. "Yes," they whispered in unison.

"What is that over there?" Patricia's husband asked, holding a squalling Isabella in his arms.

"I'm not sure. I didn't see it, at first glance, but it seems to be a small quilt of some kind." Patricia walked around to the far side of the tree. "Is it for a doll?" she asked. "I've never seen it before, but whoever did it, was meticulous. It's exquisitely done."

Abigail felt her knees tremble, as her eyes filled with unshed tears. She could barely breather. It couldn't be true. "Let me see it," she requested. Before she touched it, she knew another miracle had occurred. She hadn't seen the precious quilt since the day her mother ran back into the house, trying desperately to save her quilt pieces from the consuming flames. Holding it close to her cheek, she could smell her old home—a faint scent of lilacs from her mother, and the endearing scent of her father's tobacco. "It was mine," she muttered softly. "It was my blanket when I was an infant. My mother stitched it out of scraps. I haven't seen it in more than forty years."

Suddenly, without any coaxing, Abigail felt the urge to fold its colorful patches around her fretful granddaughter. Instantly, the child ceased her wailing, and pressed her tiny face against the softness of the quilt. Everyone was stunned into silence.

Joshua was the first to speak. "If I hadn't seen it with my own two eyes, I never would have believed it. Come to think of it... there is a lot here, that defies explanation, and it all started with that little boy."

"Boy?" Patricia asked.

Abigail tells them all about the strange and remarkable child she found on her porch, half starved and nearly frozen to within an inch of his life. "His hair was the color of a cloud, and his eyes were as lustrous as raindrops. He didn't speak, but when he smiled, my heart melted. I would have done anything for him. If I live to be one hundred, I don't reckon I'll ever understand what has happened here, this night."

"It's Christmas, Mama," her daughter reminded her. "It's a time for miracles."

"It is at that." With happy tears rolling down her cheeks, Abigail's attention was suddenly drawn upward. "Oh, look at that," she exclaimed. A beautiful, flaxen-haired angel graced the tip of the highest branch on the tree. The little angel, with enormous blue eyes, so pale they almost appeared silver, was smiling down at her. "Merry Christmas and many more to come", he seemed to be saying silently. Abigail's heart skipped a beat, and a warm feeling flooded her body, as if she'd been touched by the hand of the Almighty.

"Luke stopped by for a holiday visit and changed my life. Someday, I may explain it to you; but for now, let's go into the kitchen and have some pie and coffee, with cookies and hot chocolate for Connor."

"But Mama," her daughter retorted, "there's nothing for you under that tree. You didn't receive a present."

Abigail Rose looked up into the loving eyes of the man with whom she had been in love, so many years ago, and smiled.

"That's where you're wrong, dear. "I received the best gift of all—the gift of Christmas, all year through."

The End

A NOTE FROM THE AUTHOR

Many of the events told in this story, are indeed factual. It is true that in the November election of 1860, not one vote from Vernon County was cast for Mr. Abraham Lincoln; and in 1861, a Vernon County battalion was formed to fight at the Battle of Wilson Creek, which went on to be a decisive victory for the South.

It is also true that by 1863, crime and violence had become an everyday way of life for the people living in this quiet, Missouri town. Surrounded by Kansas Jayhawkers to the west, and the Cedar County militia, the citizenry were preyed upon regularly. But it wasn't until the Federal militia declared Nevada City to be a bastion of lawlessness, and a safe-haven for "Bushwhackers", did they face their biggest challenge.

On the morning of May 25, 1863, orders were given to kill all Bushwhackers, and burn every building to the ground. Residents were given twenty minutes to gather their belongings, before their homes were torched. In total, seventy-five homes and businesses were destroyed that day —less than a dozen were spared. For the remainder of the war, soldiers would pass through and remark, "This is where Nevada City once stood."

The town did not attempt to rebuild until several years after the conclusion of the war. Then in 1868, with the help of hard-working immigrants, the town rose up from the ashes and was incorporated a year later. In 1869, they chose to drop 'city' from the name, and it became simply, Nevada, Missouri.

Nevada now boasts a Bushwhacker Museum and Jail, and is widely regarded as having one of the best small town collections in the Midwest.

You may visit their website.

http://www.bushwhacker.org/

ABOUT THE AUTHOR

Alice Addy

Alice Addy is at her very best when writing a charming and enduring holiday novel, Keeping with the Christmas spirit, all her stories are filled with hope, love, and the magic of the season. It is, of course, that time of year when we allow all our childish wishes and dreams to run free, filling our hearts and minds with wondrous images. Even the familiar holiday aromas, drifting through the air, fill our lungs with sweet memories of our past. We remember what it was like, so many years ago, celebrating with family and friends. Perhaps it was one special tree, standing tall against the wall and sparkling with the twinkling lights your father struggled to untangle. Maybe you remember sneaking down the stairs to see a shiny red bicycle peeking out from behind a tower of wrapped presents. Or it could be the last sweet time you sat around the piano singing carols with your precious grandmother. Whatever your favorite memory, Alice paints a poignant picture with her words, making each page come to life in your imagination.

With each and every holiday story Alice writes, she wishes her reader a most wonderful and joyous celebration.

BOOKS BY ALICE ADDY

Courage Series — Historical

MISSOURI LEGEND
ARIZONA JUSTICE
PENNSYLVANIA VALOR

Birdsong Series — Historical

TRACKS TO LOVE
SWEETWATER
BONJOUR, MY WIFE
IT'S ONLY THE BEGINNING

Holiday Series

CASH FOR CHRISTMAS
A VISIT FROM NICK

Ladies of the Night Series – Paranormal

DARK SIDE OF REDEMPTION
SEEKING REDEMPTION

Visit Alice Addy on Facebook

Made in the USA
Columbia, SC
27 December 2021